CHOPPED-UP BIRDY'S FEET

Books by Todd Strasser

Help! I'm Trapped in the First Day
of Summer Camp
Help! I'm Trapped in My Sister's Body
Help! I'm Trapped in the President's Body
Help! I'm Trapped in My Gym Teacher's Body
Howl-A-Ween
Help! I'm Trapped in Obedience School
Abe Lincoln for Class President
Help! I'm Trapped in the First Day of School
Please Don't Be Mine, Julie Valentine
Help! I'm Trapped in My Teacher's Body
The Diving Bell
The Lifeguards
How I Changed My Life
Free Willy
Jumanji
Home Alone
Home Alone II: Lost in New York
The Accident
The Mall from Outer Space
Girl Gives Birth to Own Prom Date

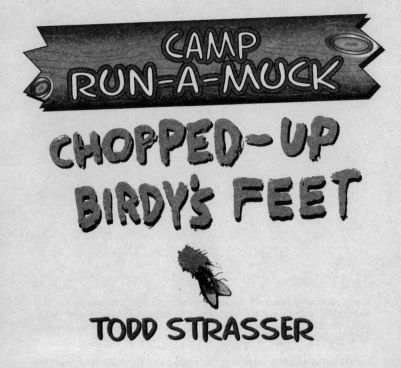

CAMP RUN-A-MUCK

CHOPPED-UP BIRDY'S FEET

TODD STRASSER

AN
APPLE
PAPERBACK

SCHOLASTIC INC.
New York Toronto London Auckland Sydney

ISBN 0-590-74263-9

12 11 10 9 8 7 6 5 4 3 2 1   7 8 9/9 0 1 2/0

Printed in the U.S.A.
First Scholastic printing, June 1997

*To Charlie and Brad Jacobson,
a couple of cool campers.*

CHOPPED-UP BIRDY'S FEET

"**A** day off," my good buddy Justin said. "Can you believe it? We don't have to spend the day sweating our butts off in that hot kitchen."

Justin and I were sitting on the front steps of the bunkhouse. The reason we had the day off was that the whole camp was taking a field trip and wouldn't be back until late that night. The morning sun was rising in the sky, burning the dew off the grassy lawns of Camp Run-a-Muck. It was going to be hot.

Bag Jammer and the orphan Sherpas were just coming back from their early morning jog. Bag was a big, muscular Sherpa from Tibet. The orphans followed him everywhere in a single-file line.

"This is being a rare and wonderful day," Bag said, wiping the sweat from his forehead.

Terry Thomas, wearing a blue-and-white-striped

1

bathrobe, came out onto the front steps and stretched in the warm sunlight. *Urrrrruuuupppp!* He let out a deep, long belch.

"Nice one, Terry," Justin said.

"Thanks," Terry replied. "Nothing like a good burp first thing in the morning."

Terry was a tall, thin black guy, the Chief Cook at Camp Run-a-Muck and our boss. "What are you guys gonna do with your day off?"

I could feel the hot sun on my arms and head. "Anyone feel like a swim in the lake?"

"Sounds good," said Justin. "Want to ask Amanda?"

I nodded, not surprised by the suggestion. Justin was in love with Amanda Kirby and always wanted to include her in our plans.

We went back into the bunkhouse and got our bathing suits. Then we headed across the camp toward the animal hut. Amanda ran the camp canteen, but she spent most of her free time taking care of the animals in the animal hut.

"Know what, Lucas?" Justin said as we walked past the campers' cabins. "It's so beautiful out today that I may finally get up the nerve to ask Amanda for a date."

"Yeah, right." I didn't believe him. Justin must've said the same thing a hundred times, but he always chickened out.

"No, really," Justin insisted. "I mean it."

Suddenly I stopped. "Am I seeing things, or is that Brad Schmook on The Blob's private golf course?"

Justin squinted into the distance. "You're right!"

CHAPTER

2

Brad Schmook was not our favorite person. He was The Blob's personal caddie, gofer, and a total creep. Since Justin and I worked in the kitchen, we'd had no choice but to feed him things like live chocolate-covered flies, mutilated monkey meat kebab, and greasy grimy gopher gutburgers.

"Let's go see what he's up to," I said.

We took a detour from the animal hut and headed toward The Blob's private golf course. The Blob was Bob Kirby, the owner of Camp Run-a-Muck. He really didn't care about the camp. The only reason the camp existed was to make enough money to pay for his private golf course, which The Blob ran for himself and his friends.

As we walked toward the course, we watched Brad drop to his hands and knees on the green around the first hole.

"What's he doing?" Justin asked.

"Got me," I replied.

After a few moments, we got close enough to see that Brad was cutting the grass around the first hole with scissors. His face was red and sunburned. Sweat ran down his forehead and dripped off his nose.

"Yo, Brad!" Justin called out. "Are you mental?"

Brad looked up with a surprised expression. "What are you guys doing here?"

"That's what we want to ask you," Justin said. "Don't you know you're not allowed on The Blob's private golf course?"

"And haven't you ever heard of a lawn mower?" I asked.

"Mr. Kirby says I have to cut this green by hand," Brad grumbled, wiping his forehead.

"So why not use a lawn mower?" I asked.

"He wants it to be perfect." Brad didn't look happy.

"Why?" Justin asked.

"He has a deal with the Defungo Company," Brad explained. "They're holding a million-dollar hole-in-one contest here next week."

"Defungo Extra-Strength Deep-Pit Deodorant?" Justin said.

"Right." Brad nodded.

"How does it work?" I asked.

"You just rub it into your armpits to get rid of that deep-pit odor," Brad said.

"No, I meant how does the *contest* work?" I said.

"Oh," Brad said. "You get ten tries. If anyone gets a hole in one, they win a million bucks. *And* they get to appear in a year's worth of Defungo Extra-Strength Deep-Pit Deodorant ads."

"Wow, I'm gonna do that," Justin said with a smile. "I wouldn't mind winning a million dollars."

"Can *anyone* enter the contest?" I asked.

"Anyone who can come up with the hundred-dollar entry fee," Brad said.

Justin's smile faded into a look of disappointment. "Aw, man, there's always a catch. I can't come up with a hundred bucks. What about you, Lucas?"

I shook my head. Out on the fairway to the first hole, some big black-and-white birds were wandering around. "What about them?" I asked. "Are they in the contest?"

Brad shook his head. "Those Canadian geese just showed up yesterday. All they do is hang around the golf course eating the grass. They're a real pain."

"Because they get in the way?" Justin guessed.

"The real problem is goose poop," Brad said. "It gets all over the golf balls and turns them green. Anyway, once you pay the hundred-dollar entry fee, you can practice on the course as much as you want."

"Right." Justin nodded sourly. "No one will wonder where *you'll* get the entry fee. You'll use the money you got by ripping off campers."

"But — " Brad started to say.

"It figures," Justin continued in a disgusted tone. "Schmook the Crook scores again."

"That's not — " Brad tried to say.

"The only silver lining of this cloud is that you'll never get that hole in one," Justin went on. "You'll see, man. In the long run, crime doesn't pay."

The look on Brad's face hardened. Justin had really made him mad.

Justin turned to me. "Come on, Lucas, let's get out of here."

We started to walk away.

"Go ahead back to your dumb camp!" Brad yelled behind us. "But you'd better enjoy it while you can because pretty soon Mr. Kirby is gonna bulldoze the whole thing."

Justin and I stopped and turned around. "What are you talking about?"

"Mr. Kirby's getting rid of the camp after this summer," Brad said. "He's gonna build a couple more golf courses and turn this whole place into one big golf resort."

"Bull," I said.

"If you don't believe me, go ask Terry," Brad replied.

CHAPTER

3

Justin and I headed back to the bunkhouse.

"Brad's such a liar," Justin said. But then he gave me a worried look. "You think he's lying, don't you?"

"We'll know as soon as we find Terry," I said.

"Wouldn't that be a bummer?" Justin asked. "I mean, I know The Blob makes us work too hard, and the food's totally disgusting, and the camp's completely disorganized. But the truth is, I really like it here."

"Yeah," I had to agree. "No matter how bad it gets, it's still fun."

Back at the bunkhouse, Terry was sitting on the front steps, getting some sun and reading a book called *Alive*. Terry was always reading weird books.

"What's this one about?" Justin asked.

"A rugby team," Terry replied. "Their plane crashes high in the Andes Mountains in Chile."

"Oh, yeah," Justin said. "I saw that movie. The

8

guys run out of food, so they start eating the bodies of their buddies who died in the crash."

"I figured maybe I could pick up some good recipes," Terry said, with a slightly sinister smile.

Justin and I nodded uncertainly. With Terry, you never knew whether he was kidding or not. Just a few weeks before, he'd been reading a book about some Norwegian dudes who ate their dogs on the way back from the South Pole.

"I thought you guys were going down to the waterfront to take a swim," Terry said.

"We were," said Justin. "But we ran into Schmook the Crook, and he told us this totally bogus story about The Blob wanting to bulldoze the camp and build a golf resort. That's like total horse manure, right?"

Terry sighed reluctantly. "I'm afraid not, Justin."

"You mean it's true!?" Justin gasped.

Terry nodded. "I just found out the other day. I didn't want to tell you guys because I figured you'd be really bummed."

"That stinks!" Justin put his hands on his hips and stomped around for a moment. Then he looked back at Terry. "You think there's any way we could get The Blob to change his mind?"

"I don't know," Terry said. "Why don't you go ask him?"

CHAPTER

"**Y**ou're not serious," I said to Justin. Once again we were walking across the camp.

"Better believe I am," Justin said. "This camp means too much to too many kids to let The Blob destroy it."

"You're really going to talk to The Blob?" I asked.

"I have to, Lucas," Justin said gravely. "Camp Run-a-Muck is a national treasure. Do you have any idea what goes on at *other* camps?"

"The kids probably eat better food," I said.

"True," said Justin. "But they also have to *do* stuff. They have to swim in freezing-cold lakes. And they have to take sports like tennis and roller hockey. And they have to go to sing-alongs and participate in color wars. Camp Run-a-Muck is probably the only camp left where a kid can go with the comfort of knowing that *no one is going to make him do anything.*"

"Wait a minute," I said. "I don't believe you really care about that. I think you're just worried that if Camp Run-a-Muck closes, you'll never get to see Amanda again."

"Shhhh!" Justin quickly pressed a finger to his lips and whispered, "Here she comes now."

CHAPTER

5

Amanda waved and came toward us, her blond hair bobbing on her shoulders and a smile on her face. "Hey, guys, what are you up to?"

It always seemed like she smiled a second longer at me than at Justin.

"We're going to see your uncle," I said. Bob "The Blob" Kirby was Amanda's step-uncle.

"What for?" Amanda asked.

Justin told her how The Blob wanted to turn Camp Run-a-Muck into a golf resort.

"I'm glad we ran into you," he said. "I was hoping you'd come with us. Maybe you could help us change your uncle's mind."

"I'll go with you," Amanda said. "But don't expect any miracles."

The Blob lived in a big yellow-and-white house on a hill behind the camp, and near the first hole of his private golf course.

Grrrrroooooofff! As we neared the house, The Blob Dog barked meanly. The Blob Dog was a fat, nasty bulldog, not unlike The Blob himself.

Justin slowed down. "Every time I hear that dog bark, I think of the night he almost had us for dinner."

"If The Blob shuts down Camp Run-a-Muck, The Blob Dog is one thing you won't miss," I said.

"Better believe it," Justin agreed.

We reached The Blob's front door, and Amanda knocked.

"Who is it?" The Blob's voice grumbled from inside.

"Amanda," his niece replied.

A moment later the front door opened, and there stood The Blob. His big, round, bald head shined in the sun as he squinted his beady little eyes. His huge, bulging stomach stretched his bright pink polo shirt to the limit as it hung over his bright yellow golf slacks. In his hand was a black garbage bag.

When he saw Amanda, he smiled. But when he saw Justin and me, he frowned.

"Is it true that you're planning to close the camp and turn it into a golf resort?" Amanda asked.

Deep furrows appeared in The Blob's forehead. "Why, yes, that is true."

"Why?" Amanda asked.

"Because I love golf and I hate all those noisy, whiny little campers," he replied.

Amanda looked at us and shrugged as if to say, "There's your answer."

"Just out of curiosity," I said. "Is there anything we could do to change your mind?"

The Blob rubbed his chin and thought. "If you really don't want me to shut down Run-a-Muck, you could buy the camp from me."

"How much?" Justin asked.

The Blob grinned. "One million dollars."

CHAPTER

"**A**nyone know how to come up with a million dollars?" Justin asked as we walked with Amanda toward the waterfront.

"Win the hole-in-one contest," I said.

"Fat chance." Justin scoffed at the idea. "I don't even know how to play golf. Either of you play?"

Amanda and I shook our heads.

Justin held up the black garbage bag. Just before we left The Blob's house, The Blob ordered him to take it and get rid of it. Inside was a dead goose that had gotten ka-bonged in the head by a golf ball.

"We went to save the camp and came back with a dead goose," Justin said wistfully.

"What a way to go," I said. "I mean, you're just waddling along, eating grass, making goose poops, and basically minding your own business, then *Wham!* you get smacked in the head with a golf ball."

15

"I think it's terrible," said Amanda, the animal lover. "Either he should find a way to get the geese off the golf course, or they should stop playing until the geese leave."

"That reminds me of a joke," Justin said.

I stopped and looked at my watch. "Ten thirty-five. A new record!"

"What are you talking about?" Justin asked.

"It's ten thirty-five in the morning and you're telling your first joke of the day," I explained. "You haven't told a joke since last night. That's the longest you've gone all summer without telling a joke."

"So what do you call a cow with two legs?" Justin asked.

"What does that have to do with a dead goose?" I asked.

"Geese, cows, they're all farm animals," Justin said. "So, can you guess the answer?"

Amanda and I shook our heads. I was surprised, because Amanda was usually pretty good at figuring out Justin's jokes.

"I think you've finally stumped me," she said.

A big grin appeared on Justin's face. "The answer is lean beef."

"Huh?" Neither Amanda nor I got it.

"Think about it," Justin said. "If a cow has only two legs, it has to lean on something to stand up, right? And beef comes from cows."

"Steers, actually," I corrected him.

"So the beef from a cow that leans is lean beef," Justin explained.

Amanda rolled her eyes. "Sure, Justin."

"So what do you call a cow with no legs?" Justin asked.

This time Amanda refused to give up. "Uh, ground beef?"

"Unbelievable." Justin shook his head in amazed admiration. We started to walk again. "Any ideas about what to do with the dead goose?"

"After we take a swim we could give it to Roadkill Man," I said.

"Good idea," said Justin. "And then we could keep going and have lunch at Log Cabin Pizza."

CHAPTER

7

After our swim we dried off and started through the woods. Roadkill Man lived in a cave with his wife, Mrs. Roadkill Man.

"I bet Roadkill Man's gonna be pretty happy with this goose," Justin said. "You know how sick he is of squashed skunk and greasy gopher."

"Not only that," I said. "But the goose wasn't hit by a car, or run over by a truck like most of the stuff he eats. So it should be in pretty good shape for cooking."

As we got deeper into the woods, the canopy of trees shaded us from the heat of the sun. It was quiet and still with a few shafts of bright light where the sun managed to sneak through the leaves.

"All these trees remind me of a joke," Justin said.

I turned to Amanda and pretended to be surprised. "Can you believe it? Justin wants to tell a joke."

18

"Amazing." Amanda also pretended to be surprised.

"Very funny, guys," Justin deadpanned. "So how do you catch a squirrel?"

Neither Amanda nor I could guess.

"You climb up a tree and act like a nut," Justin said.

Amanda grimaced.

"Don't you *ever* get tired of telling lame jokes?" I asked Justin.

"Hey, listen," Justin said. "*Anyone* can tell a good joke. That doesn't take any skill at all. You just tell the joke and people laugh. What really takes skill is telling a bad joke and still making people laugh."

"Well, I hate to say this, Justin," said Amanda. "But you still need to work on your skills."

"Fore!" A voice rang through the forest. Justin, Amanda, and I stopped and looked around.

"Did someone just yell 'fore'?" I asked.

"Four what?" Justin asked.

"Isn't that what golfers say before they hit the ball?" asked Amanda.

"In the *forest*?" I said.

Poing! Something ricocheted off a tree near us.

Justin, Amanda, and I instantly ducked.

Boink! It hit another tree.

Doing! And another.

Plink! With a metallic sound it fell into a hole in the ground near us.

We went over to see what it was. Justin kneeled down and reached into the hole.

"It's a golf ball," he said, holding up the ball. "It looks like someone buried a tin cup in the ground here."

"You think whoever hit the ball was actually trying to get it in the cup?" Amanda asked.

"Either that or it's the most amazing coincidence I've ever seen," Justin said.

"But who would even think of playing golf in a forest?" I wondered out loud.

We heard a rustling sound coming toward us through the underbrush. Looking around, I caught a glimpse between the trees of a tangled mess of greasy gray hair held in place by a sweat-stained bandanna. The strong, tart scent of B.O. wafted through the air, burning our noses and stinging our eyes.

"It's Roadkill Man," I said.

CHAPTER

Roadkill Man came through the woods wearing colorful hippie beads and tattered, worn-out hippie clothes. He was carrying an old wooden golf club over his shoulder. When he saw us he grinned, revealing his missing teeth, and gave us the peace sign.

"Hi, Roadkill Man," we greeted him, wiping the burning tears from our eyes. Roadkill Man probably had the strongest B.O. known to man.

"Hey, guys, how's it going?" Roadkill Man asked. "Anyone see a golf ball?"

"Like this?" Justin held up the ball he'd just found.

"That's the one," Roadkill Man said. He pointed at the tin cup buried in the ground. "How far was I from the cup?"

"You were in it," Justin replied.

"Far out!" Roadkill Man exclaimed. "A hole in one!"

"You play golf in the woods?" I asked in disbelief.

"Where else am I supposed to play?" Roadkill Man asked back.

He had a good point. The Blob had the only golf course in the area. And there was no way in the world he would ever allow a grunge like Roadkill Man onto his private course.

"How long have you been playing?" Amanda asked.

"All my life," Roadkill Man said. "My dad was a golf pro. I basically grew up on a golf course."

"But how can you play in the woods?" Justin asked. "I mean, with all the tree trunks and branches and undergrowth in the way."

"It's not easy," Roadkill Man admitted. "But you learn to adapt. You learn to bank your shots off the tree trunks. It's like playing pool."

"That's awesome," Justin said, then remembered the bag he was carrying. "Hey, Roadkill Man. We brought you some dinner. It's a goose that got bonked on the head by a golf ball."

"That's very kind of you," Roadkill Man said. "Mrs. Roadkill Man will appreciate it."

"How's she doing?" Amanda asked.

"Well, funny you should ask," Roadkill Man said. "It just so happens that she's gonna have a baby."

I felt my jaw drop. "Roadkill Baby!"

Roadkill Man beamed like a proud father. "That's right."

"That's great news," Justin said. He reached forward to pat Roadkill Man on the back, then thought better of it and stopped himself.

"You must be really excited," said Amanda, wiping the tears from her eyes.

"I sure am," Roadkill Man replied. "But you don't have to cry."

"Oh, uh, those are just tears of joy," Amanda said. Actually, they were tears caused by stinging B.O.

"Well, I'm pretty joyful, too," Roadkill Man said. "But I'm also worried. You know, for years Mrs. Roadkill Man and I have lived happily here in the forest, eating roadkill and watching TV and stuff. It's been an easy life. But a baby is gonna complicate things."

"You mean, it's going to take up a lot of your time?" Justin guessed.

"And money," Roadkill Man added. "We're gonna have to get diapers and bottles and baby formula. There's trips to the pediatrician and food store. I mean, you can't expect an infant to just start out eating roadkill. It takes a while for the digestive system to get used to road tar and engine oil."

"What are you going to do?" Amanda asked.

"I'm gonna have to get into a capitalist trip and earn some money," Roadkill Man said. "I hate to say it, but I may actually have to take a regular job."

Roadkill Man winced as he said that. I couldn't help feeling bad for him. He'd probably never had a regular job in his whole life. Then I looked at the golf club resting on his shoulder.

Suddenly I had an idea!

CHAPTER

"**M**aybe you won't have to get a regular job," I said.

"Why not?" Roadkill Man asked.

"You just got a hole in one here in the woods," I said. "How often does that happen?"

"Oh, every now and then," he said.

"If you can get a hole in one here, I bet it wouldn't be too hard to get one on a regular golf course where there are no trees in the way," I said.

"Well, I haven't tried it in a long time." Roadkill Man stroked his long gray beard thoughtfully. "But it makes sense."

"You mean, Roadkill Man could enter the hole-in-one contest?" Justin said, catching on.

"Exactly," I said.

"Then he'd never have to worry about money again," Amanda said.

"Hey, I like the sound of that," said Roadkill Man.

"But what about Camp Run-a-Muck?" Justin asked.

"I was just about to get to that," I said, turning to Roadkill Man. "Here's the deal. We'll get you the money to enter the contest. But in return, you have to agree that if you win, you'll use the million dollars to buy Camp Run-a-Muck."

"Why would I want to do that?" Roadkill Man asked.

"Because if you don't, The Blob is going to bulldoze the camp and build a golf resort," I said.

"Hey, that reminds me of a joke," Justin said.

"Not now," I said. "I'm having a serious conversation with Roadkill Man."

"Oh, please?" Justin begged.

"No!"

"Oh, come on," Justin whined. "It'll only take a second. We could spend more time arguing than it'll take to tell it."

I gave in. "Oh, okay, tell your joke."

"What do you call a sleeping cow?" Justin asked.

"A bulldozer!" Amanda, Roadkill Man, and I shouted at him all at once.

Justin grinned sheepishly. "Guess it was pretty obvious, huh?"

I turned back to Roadkill Man. "Want to know what'll happen once The Blob builds his golf resort? Pretty soon he'll start building condominiums and shopping malls. And before you know it, all the animals around here will be driven away. Instead of eating nice fresh roadkill, you'll be fishing your meals out of restaurant garbage cans."

Roadkill Man made a face. "That sounds terrible."

"You want a boy or girl baby?" Justin asked.

"Uh, a cute little baby girl would be nice," Roadkill Man said.

"Well, think of this," said Justin. "When your baby daughter grows up, they won't call her Roadkill Girl. They'll have to call her Garbage Can Girl."

"Mrs. Roadkill Man would hate that," Roadkill Man said.

"That's why you have to buy Camp Run-a-Muck if you win the contest," I said.

"But what would I do with a camp?" Roadkill Man asked.

"You wouldn't have to do *anything* with it," I said. "All you'd have to do is live there and charge kids to come in the summer."

"And you could spend all the money you get on your daughter," Amanda added.

"Sounds too good to pass up," Roadkill Man said. "Okay, I'll enter the contest."

CHAPTER 10

We left Roadkill Man in the woods and continued to the main road. Soon we arrived at Log Cabin Pizza, where we ordered a brick-oven pie and a big bottle of Coke.

"Man, this is gonna be great!" Justin raved while I cut everyone a slice from the pizza. "We're gonna save Camp Run-a-Muck and get rid of The Blob at the same time! Then we'll be able to give the campers good food every day instead of leftovers and American chop suey."

"Unless Roadkill Man decides they should all eat roadkill," Amanda quipped.

"No way," Justin insisted. "From now on it'll all be good fresh food. Like this pizza. Man, I don't know how I'd survive if I couldn't get a good slice with a crispy crust like this once in a while."

"Know what would be cool?" I said. "If Roadkill Man buys the camp, maybe we could get him to put a couple of brick ovens in the kitchen. Then we could have pizza like this all the time."

"Just think of it," Amanda said dreamily. "A camp where you don't have to do anything and you can have pizza any time you like."

"Sounds like the best camp in the world," I said, holding up a slice. "Crispy crust, fresh tomato sauce . . ."

"Which reminds me — " Justin began.

"It must be time for a joke," Amanda finished the sentence for him.

Justin looked surprised. "How'd you know?"

"I guess I'm just psychic," Amanda said, and gave me a wink.

"So why was the tomato blushing?" Justin asked.

Amanda and I shook our heads.

"He saw the salad dressing," Justin said.

Amanda and I groaned.

"I want you to do me a favor, Justin," I said. "Once Roadkill Man buys Camp Run-a-Muck, you have to promise to limit the number of jokes you tell a day."

"*If* Roadkill Man buys Camp Run-a-Muck," Amanda reminded us. "First he has to win the hole-in-one contest. And before he can even enter the contest, we have to come up with the hundred-dollar entry fee."

Justin slurped up the last of his soda. "I forgot about that. How are we gonna get the bucks?"

"We're gonna have to borrow it," I said.

"From who?" Amanda asked.

"Who do we know who might have money?" I asked back.

"Terry, Bag, and the orphan Sherpas," Justin said.

We'd finished our pizza. I stood up. "Okay, guys, it's time to do some fund-raising."

CHAPTER

11

We tried Terry first. He was still sitting on the steps of the bunkhouse when we got back to camp. In one hand was that *Alive* book. In the other hand was an egg-and-bacon sandwich he must have rustled up in the camp kitchen.

"Hey, Terry, how's it going?" Justin asked.

Terry didn't answer or look up from the book. He just nodded.

"Must be a really interesting book," Justin said.

Terry bit into the sandwich and chewed.

"So how did they do it?" Justin asked. "I mean, did they just build a fire and cook up one of the dead guys?"

Terry shook his head. "No fire."

A shocked expression grew on Justin's face. "You mean, they ate the guys . . . raw?"

Terry shook his head again. "They were way up in the mountains in the crashed plane. During the day, the sun came out and made the metal on the outside of the plane really hot. So they cut strips of flesh and put it on the metal to dry. Then they'd eat it."

"I'm sorry." Amanda made a face. "But that is the absolute most grossest thing I've ever heard."

"Grosser than Brad eating live chocolate-covered flies?" Justin asked.

"Yes," said Amanda.

"*Uurrp!*" Terry belched and took another bite of his sandwich. "They were starving. They would have died if they hadn't eaten something."

"I agree with Amanda, it's still gross!" Justin stuck out his tongue and looked like he wanted to barf. "They all sat in a circle and ate a dead guy?"

Terry sighed and closed the book. "No, they didn't sit in a circle. Most of them were just as grossed out by the idea as you are. I mean, starvation is an incredible motivator. It'll warp your mind in no time. It started out with a couple of guys doing it alone with just a little body part."

"You mean, like a hand or something?" Justin asked.

"Something like that." Terry took another bite of his sandwich.

"You know, that reminds me of a joke," Justin said.

"Why am I *not* surprised?" I moaned wearily.

"Where do people with one hand shop?" Justin asked.

No one knew the answer.

"In the secondhand store," Justin said.

Terry squinted at him. "Tell me, Justin, is there a *reason* why you're standing here annoying me on my day off?"

"Well, actually there is," Justin said. Then he told Terry about the Defungo $1 Million Hole-in-One Contest.

"Defungo Extra-Strength Deep-Pit Deodorant?" Terry asked.

"Right," said Justin.

"How does it work?" Terry asked.

"You just rub it into your armpits to get rid of that deep-pit odor," Justin said.

"No, I meant how does the *contest* work?" Terry said.

Justin explained how if someone got a hole in one, they'd win a million dollars and get to appear in a year's worth of Defungo Extra-Strength Deep-Pit Deodorant ads.

"The only problem is we need one hundred dollars so Roadkill Man can enter the contest," he added.

Terry blinked. "Are you feeling okay?"

"Uh, I think so," Justin replied. "Why?"

"Why?" Terry raised an eyebrow. "Because it's next to impossible to get a hole in one. Most golfers are lucky to do it *once* in their lifetimes."

"But Roadkill Man does it all the time," Justin said, and explained how Roadkill Man played golf in the woods and banked the balls off trees.

"He golfs in *the woods*?" Terry repeated in disbelief.

Justin, Amanda, and I nodded. Terry stared at us like we were nuts. Then he looked back at his book and started to read again.

"I get the feeling Terry isn't interested," I said.

"Time to try Bag," said Justin.

"**M**aybe we *are* crazy to think Roadkill Man could make a hole in one," Justin said as we went looking for Bag and the orphan Sherpas.

"But it's the only chance we have," said Amanda.

"That's no chance at all if we can't get someone to come up with the entry fee," I said, looking around. "Where are those guys, anyway?"

"There." Justin pointed toward the batting cages. The camp had three batting cages with pitching machines, where kids could practice hitting. One of the machines was set to throw medium-speed pitches, another to throw fast, and the third to throw super fast.

As Justin, Amanda, and I walked toward them, we could see Bag with the six orphan Sherpas. Originally, the orphans were supposed to spend the summer at Camp Run-a-Muck before going back to Tibet. But The Blob had double-crossed them, and now they didn't have the money to fly home. Bag had decided that if the Sherpas had to stay here, he would Americanize them by teaching them to speak English and play baseball.

The trouble was, Bag didn't know much about either.

"What in the world are they doing?" Justin asked.

It appeared that instead of using the batting cages for batting practice, the orphan Sherpas were using them for *catching* practice. That seemed to work okay in the medium-speed cage, and even in the fast-speed cage. But the super-fast-speed cage was another story. The orphan Sherpas weren't very big. Each time one of them tried to catch a super-high-speed pitch, he was knocked off his feet and thrown backwards into the fence at the back of the cage.

Thwamp! The speeding ball would smash into the waiting Sherpa.

Crash! The Sherpa would sail backwards and hit the fence. Then he would crumple to the ground and have to be dragged out of the cage by the other orphans.

Justin, Amanda, and I walked over to the batting cages.

Thwamp! Crash! Another orphan Sherpa was knocked silly in the super-fast cage.

"Hello, my friends." Bag gave us a big smile. "I am being glad you are here to see how the orphans are learning the great American sport of baseball."

Thwamp! Crash! Yet another orphan Sherpa was knocked silly in the super-fast cage. We watched his pals drag him out.

"Uh, Bag, I think we need to talk," I said.

Bag scowled. "Is something being wrong, Lucas?"

"Well, sort of," I said. "You see, those are *batting* cages, not *catching* cages. The orphans are supposed to be hitting those balls, not trying to catch them."

"Oh!" Bag looked as if he suddenly understood something that had been puzzling him. He pointed at the super-fast cage. "Maybe that is explaining why the orphans are having such a hard time catching these balls."

Thwamp! Crash! Another semiconscious orphan Sherpa was dragged out of the cage by his pals.

"Listen, why don't you have them stop, anyway," I said. "We need to talk to all of you."

Bag yelled something in Tibetan at the orphan Sherpas, who limped and staggered over to us. It appeared that every one of them had tried to catch a super-fast pitch, because they all had black eyes, bleeding noses, and split lips.

Once again, Justin told the story of The Blob's plan to turn Camp Run-a-Muck into a golf resort, and how our only chance to save the camp was to get one hundred dollars to send Roadkill Man to the Defungo Extra-Strength Deep-Pit Deodorant Hole-in-One Contest.

"How does it work?" Bag asked.

"If you get a hole in one, you win the million dollars," I explained.

"No, I meant how does the deodorant work?" Bag asked.

Justin explained how you rubbed it into your armpits to get rid of body odor.

"This is being very interesting," Bag said. "I have never heard of this thing called deodorant before."

"We've noticed," Amanda said with a crooked smile.

Bag gathered the orphan Sherpas around him, and they whispered in Tibetan.

"Why are they whispering?" Amanda wondered out loud. "We can't understand them, anyway."

Bag turned to us. "We are being interested in trying some of this deodorant. This is something many Americans are using, correct?"

"Yeah, Bag," Justin said. "But we're not talking about deodorant now. We're talking about the hundred-dollar entry fee for the contest."

Bag shook his head. "I am being sorry, but we are not having the money. You see, this Blob is not paying us what he promised. However, we would love to be getting some free samples of deodorant if this Roadkill Man can win the contest."

"Well, I hate to say this," I said. "But if we don't come up with the money, Roadkill Man won't even be in the contest."

Bag nodded glumly. "Then we are being sorry to disappoint you."

Amanda, Justin, and I headed back toward the bunkhouse.

"Well, I guess that just about kills that idea," Justin said.

"What about the campers?" Amanda asked. "Could we ask them for the money?"

"We could," I said, "but they're all broke after Brad the Cad forced them to spend all their money on his rip-off candy."

"If there was one thing I could change about this summer, it would be him," Justin said.

"Not the bad food?" Amanda asked.

"Hey, like Roadkill Man said, you can get used to bad food after a while," Justin replied. "The thing I'll never get used to are sneaky, low-life dirt-balls . . . like Brad Schmook."

CHAPTER 13

That night after dark the campers came back from their field trip. We were already in the bunkhouse getting ready for bed. We'd have to get up early the next morning to make breakfast for them.

Inside the bunkhouse, Terry was sitting on his bunk, reading his book.

"You guys find the money?" he asked.

Justin and I shook our heads.

"What are you going to do?" Terry asked.

"There's nothing we can do," I answered. "Roadkill Man can't enter the hole-in-one contest. He can't win a million dollars. He can't buy Camp Run-a-Muck, and The Blob will turn it into a golf resort."

"Hey, it's not the end of the world," Terry said. "Next summer we'll all get jobs in other places. The campers will just go to other camps."

"But there's no camp like this camp," Justin said sadly.

Terry nodded and started reading again.

"How are the cannibals?" Justin asked.

"They weren't cannibals," Terry said. "They were desperate, starving people who didn't want to die. It wasn't like they'd ever eat human flesh voluntarily."

"What do they call a cannibal cookbook?" Justin asked.

Terry and I shook our heads.

" *'How to Serve Your Fellow Man,'* " Justin said.

"Are you finished?" I asked.

"No," Justin answered. "How about this? When do cannibals leave the dinner table?"

"When?" I asked.

"When everyone's eaten," Justin said.

"Okay." I raised my hand in surrender. "Enough jokes."

"The thing I don't get," Justin went on, "is why didn't those rugby guys at least *cook* their buddies before they ate them?"

"Actually, that's what they started to do," Terry said. "They found some wooden crates and used them to make a fire and cooked the meat. But that actually wasn't the best thing to do, because cooking meat makes it lose a lot of its nutrients."

"Doesn't matter," Justin said.

"Can we get back to the subject?" I asked. "We were talking about saving Camp Run-a-Muck."

"Look, guys, I'm sorry this camp is gonna get bulldozed," Terry said. "But stuff like this happens all over nature. The embryos of tiger sharks fight to the death while they're still in the mother. Like, *before* they're even born. Only the survivor gets born."

"Oh, yeah?" Justin shot back. "Well, the average human produces about a quart of saliva a day. That's roughly ten thousand gallons of spit over the course of a lifetime."

Terry scratched his head. "What does *that* have to do with anything?"

Justin shrugged. "I don't know."

"Come on," I said to Justin with a yawn. "Let's go to sleep."

That night I dreamed that Roadkill Man won the million-dollar hole-in-one contest and bought Camp Run-a-Muck. But then he made all the campers collect roadkill for every meal.

"No! No! Never!" In the morning I woke up to the sound of someone screaming. In his bunk below me, Justin was twisting and thrashing and all tangled in his bedsheet.

"Hey, Justin!" I yelled. "Wake up!"

Justin opened his eyes and looked startled. "Wha——?"

"You were having a bad dream," I said.

"Better believe it," Justin said. "I dreamed I was in the camp kitchen and Terry was cutting up pieces of Brad to eat."

I noticed something green sticking out from under Justin's pillow. "Hey, what's that?"

Justin turned and saw what I was pointing at. He reached under his pillow and pulled out a wad of bills. His mouth fell open, and his eyes went wide. "It's money!"

"Serious?" I gasped.

Justin nodded and counted it. "A hundred dollars! Exactly enough for the entry fee!"

"Who put it there?" I asked.

"I don't know," Justin said. "It must've happened in the middle of the night while we were asleep."

I looked around the bunkhouse, wondering who could have put the money under Justin's pillow. Terry was sitting up in his bed, looking at us.

"Was it you?" I asked.

Terry shook his head. "No way. I can think of a lot better things to do with a hundred bucks than give it to you guys."

"It doesn't matter where the money came from," Justin said. "The only thing that matters is that now we can get Roadkill Man to enter the contest!"

CHAPTER

14

A little while later we went to the camp kitchen to make breakfast. All we had was milk, eggs, raisins, and stale bread, so we baked bread pudding.

"What do you call a blind dinosaur?" Justin asked after the orphan Sherpas served the first batch.

"It's too early for jokes," I muttered.

"Aw, come on," Justin said. "Lighten up."

"Okay," I said. "What?"

"Doyouthinkhesaurus?" Justin said.

I rolled my eyes and pulled a big bowl of bread pudding out of the oven.

"You know, this stuff isn't half bad," Justin said after tasting it. "I bet they'll ask for seconds."

I looked through the window of the kitchen door and into the dining hall. "Oh, yeah, it's going over real well with the campers."

Out in the dining hall, the campers were digging

out handfuls of the whitish pudding and throwing pudding balls at each other.

Terry joined me at the window. "Reminds me of snowball fights at Christmas."

Splat! A pudding ball slammed into the window, blocking our view.

"Looks like the orphans are going to be busy cleaning up before lunch," Terry said.

"Think Justin and I could get some time off to sign Roadkill Man up for the contest?" I asked.

Terry nodded, and we headed out of the kitchen.

A little while later we led Roadkill Man across the camp toward The Blob's golf course.

"Gee, guys, I don't know about this," Roadkill Man said uncertainly as The Blob's golf course came into view. Unlike the other golfers who lugged around heavy bags filled with clubs, Roadkill Man carried only his old wooden golf club on his shoulder.

"Oh, come on," Justin said. "Anyone who can hit a hole in one *in the woods* should have no problem hitting one on a regular golf course."

"I guess," Roadkill Man said.

"And don't forget," I added. "If you get a hole in one, you'll be set for life. You'll never have to worry about diapers and bottles for Roadkill Baby."

"That sure would be nice," Roadkill Man agreed.

When we got to the golf course, dozens of golfers were already there, practicing for the hole-in-one contest. There were so many balls flying through the air and bouncing on the grass that it looked like a hailstorm.

"Wow." Justin slowed to a halt. "Looks like a lot of people want that million-dollar prize. I never thought it would be *this* crowded."

"You can't blame them," I said, then pointed at a table with a big sign next to it. "Come on, there's the registration table. Let's go enter Roadkill Man."

We walked over to the table. The Blob was sitting there, talking and laughing with some of his golfer friends. They were all dressed in brightly colored pants and shirts. Brad the Cad was sitting nearby, polishing The Blob's golf clubs.

When The Blob and his pals saw us coming toward the registration table with Roadkill Man, the laughter stopped. The Blob narrowed his beady eyes and set his fat jaw.

"What do you want?" he asked.

"We want to enter Roadkill Man in the contest," I answered.

The Blob and his friends stared at Roadkill Man's long, tangled, greasy hair and his sweat-stained red bandanna. They stared at his colorful hippie beads and grungy leather vest and grimy bell-bottom jeans.

"Something sure smells bad," one of The Blob's friends grunted and wrinkled his nose.

"Body odor is not grounds for disqualification," Justin stated firmly.

The Blob and his friends smiled.

Then they laughed.

Pretty soon they were laughing so hard, they were all doubled over and holding their stomachs.

"Gee, people never laugh that hard when I tell a joke," Justin said.

We waited for the laughter to end. I noticed that Brad the Cad wasn't laughing. Maybe he didn't understand what The Blob and the others found so funny.

Finally The Blob stopped laughing. He took a handkerchief out of his pocket and dabbed the tears out of his eyes.

"Let me make sure I understand this," he said with a chuckle. "You want to enter that smelly old hippie and his old wooden golf club in the contest?"

"That's right." I nodded.

The Blob grinned. "Are you aware that there's a one hundred-dollar entry fee?"

Without a word I reached into my pocket and dropped the wad of bills on the table in front of him.

The Blob's face turned hard as he stared at the money. For almost a minute he didn't move. Then one of his golf buddies — a thin, tanned man with blond hair who was smoking a cigar — leaned close and spoke softly into his ear, but loud enough for us to hear.

"Look at him," the blond man said. "You really think he has a chance of getting a hole in one? Forget it! You might as well take the money."

A small smile appeared on The Blob's face. He picked up the wad of bills and counted it. "Okay, the contest is next Tuesday. Between now and then you're entitled to practice as much as you want." The smile grew larger and he added, "Not that it will make a difference."

The Blob and his friends chuckled and whispered to each other when Roadkill Man took a basket of practice balls and headed to the first tee. A flock of geese were hanging around near the tee, and when Roadkill Man arrived they started to back away and then took off into the air.

"That's weird," Justin said. "They didn't fly away when the other golfers took their practice swings."

"I guess geese have sensitive noses," I said.

Justin glanced at his watch. "I hate to say this, Lucas. But we'd better get back to the kitchen. It's time to start lunch."

"I just want to see Roadkill Man take a few practice swings," I said.

Roadkill Man stepped up to the tee and put his first practice ball on the ground. But instead of taking a swing, he stared out at the broad grassy fairway. At the end of the fairway was the first green. In the middle of the green was a thin pole with a small red flag, marking the hole.

The Blob and his friends stood behind us, watching. Someone whispered something I couldn't hear, and they all burst out in laughter. Meanwhile, Roadkill Man was still staring out at the golf course.

"How come you're not taking your practice shots?" I asked him.

"I'm just a bit freaked," Roadkill Man replied. "I mean, it's been a long time since I played on a course where you could actually *see* the hole you were aiming for."

"Don't worry, no one expects you to get a hole in one on your first shot," I said.

"No one expects you to get a hole in one, *ever*!" said the blond-haired guy. The Blob and his friends laughed again.

Roadkill Man pursed his lips and looked down at the golf ball.

He pulled his old wooden club back and over his head.

He swung.

Thwack! The ball shot up into the air.

The Blob and his friends stopped laughing.

The ball sailed straight down the fairway.

It bounced onto the green a dozen feet beyond the red flag, then rolled backwards and came to a stop about a foot from the hole.

No one spoke.

The Blob and his friends stood silently, their mouths hanging open with astonishment.

I turned back to Justin and smiled. "You're right. It's time to go back to the kitchen."

CHAPTER

16

In the camp kitchen, Justin and I helped make lunch. As usual, that meant taking all the leftovers out of the refrigerator, mixing them in a big vat of tomato sauce, and melting cheese over the top.

After lunch we had another short break and went to visit Amanda at the camp canteen. The line of campers leading to the counter was endless, since no one had been able to eat the lunch. As we walked along the line, we passed Ralphie, the red-haired champion barfer of Camp Run-a-Muck. He was waiting to buy candy with a bunch of his buddies.

"Hey, guys." Ralphie waved when he saw us. "I've got a new rating system for the food you serve. I call it the Ralphie Barf-O-Meter."

Ralphie held up a small gray box with some knobs and an antenna sticking out of it.

"How does it work?" Justin asked.

"Simple," Ralphie said. "It's based on how fast I

barf after I hear what's for lunch. The lowest score is a one. That's when I actually *eat* some of the stuff before I barf. To rate a two, all I have to do is put the stuff in my mouth and barf. A three means I *look* at the stuff and it makes me barf."

"So how did today's lunch register on the Barf-O-Meter?" Justin asked.

"Today was a four," Ralphie said. "To rate a four, I don't even have to see it. All I have to do is *smell* it."

"So that must be the highest rating," I guessed.

Ralphie shook his head. "Nope. Actually, there's a five on the Barf-O-Meter. But it's pretty rare. To rate a five, I don't have to see or smell lunch. I just have to *hear* about it and I barf."

"Wow," I said. "Have we had any fives this summer?"

"Not yet," Ralphie said. "But I know you guys can do it."

"Thanks for the vote of confidence," Justin said.

I pointed to the small gray box in Ralphie's hand. "So what is that thing, really?"

"Just the remote control for my mini Big Foot," he said. He pressed a button and turned a knob. A battery-powered orange and black toy truck with big tires shot past us on the dining room floor. "Cool, huh?"

"Very cool," I said. "You get it as a present?"

"Actually, I built it," Ralphie said.

"From a kit?" Justin asked.

"Nope, just from old toys and junk," Ralphie said.

Justin and I shared a surprised look.

"You didn't know he was a techno-genius?" asked Ricky Pulger, one of the smallest kids in camp. "Give him a couple of paper clips, a dial, and a battery and he can build almost everything."

Ralphie smiled sheepishly.

"Hey, I'll remember that," I said.

We continued down the line. Other campers made comments about lunch, but no one was really mad at us. By now they all understood that the lousy food wasn't our fault. The problem was that The Blob wouldn't spend any money to buy decent food for the campers. Instead, he spent all the food money on fancy meals for himself and his friends. He had his own private refrigerator stocked with delicacies. The refrigerator had a lock, and only The Blob and Terry had keys for it.

When we got to the front of the line, Brad was leaning on the counter while Amanda sold candy and ice cream to the campers.

"Surprise, surprise," Justin said. "Look who's here."

"Hey, guys," Brad greeted us in a friendly manner. "So I see you scraped up the money for Roadkill Man's entry fee, huh?"

Justin and I nodded. Then Justin cupped his hand around my ear and whispered, "If Brad's acting friendly, it can only mean he's up to no good."

"Brad was just telling me that you got the money," Amanda said. "Where did you get it?"

"We don't know," Justin said. "I woke up this morning, and it was under my pillow."

"An anonymous donor," Amanda said. "That's great!"

"Actually, I was wondering if maybe you were the one who left it," I said.

Amanda shook her head. "I wish, Lucas. Believe me, if I had the money, I'd give it to you."

"You really think Roadkill Man has a chance?" Brad asked.

"Why ask us?" Justin replied. "You saw how close he came to getting a hole in one in practice this morning."

"How did he get so good?" Brad asked.

"He's been playing in the woods for years," I said.

"In the woods?" Brad looked surprised. "But that's impossible. What about all the trees and junk?"

"Obviously he's developed incredible aim," Justin said.

"Amazing." Brad shook his head in awe. "And if he wins the contest, is he really gonna use the money to buy Camp Run-a-Muck from The Blob?"

"Better believe it," Justin said.

Brad just nodded and didn't say anything.

"So now that you know our plan, how come you're not scurrying back to The Blob to tell him about it?" Justin asked.

"You've got me all wrong," Brad said. "That's not what I'm into."

"Give me a break," Justin said, dismissing him.

"I'm serious," Brad insisted.

"You're seriously up to some new scam to get rich off the campers and make them suffer," Justin said. "So why don't you just bug off and go back to your evil master, The Blob."

Brad pressed his lips together and gave us an angry look. Then he left.

"What makes you so certain he's up to no good?" Amanda asked Justin once Brad had gone.

"Are you kidding?" Justin said. "The friendlier Brad acts, the nastier his plan. Believe me, you'll see."

CHAPTER

17

It wasn't long before Justin and I had to go back to the kitchen and start dinner. Terry was still reading that *Alive* book.

"Find any good recipes?" Justin asked.

Terry shook his head.

"I bet they were getting pretty good at cooking," Justin said. "Like stews and stuff?"

Terry had a grim look on his face. "No way. It got worse. First they ran out of wood for the fire. Then there was a blizzard and the plane was buried under an avalanche. They couldn't have gotten outside to start a fire even if they'd had wood."

"So what did they do?" Justin asked.

Terry shook his head slowly. "You don't want to know."

Justin gave me a look. "Wow, even Terry's grossed out. It must be really bad."

"By comparison, it makes the Camp Run-a-Muck

kitchen look like a five-star restaurant," Terry said.

"So, did you know that some elephants remain standing after they've died?" Justin asked.

Terry frowned. "Are you feeling okay?"

The kitchen door swung open, and Roadkill Man came in carrying his golf club and a black plastic garbage bag over his shoulder.

"Hey, Roadkill Man, how'd it go?" Justin asked.

"I finished practicing," he said. "But it's hot out there in the sun and I got thirsty. I was wondering if I could trouble you for some water."

"Sure thing," I said, and filled a glass for him.

"How was practice?" Justin asked. "Did you make any holes in one?"

"Not yet," Roadkill Man said. "But I'm getting pretty close. I'm starting to think I might actually be able to do it."

He put down his golf club and plastic bag and took a long drink from the glass. "Ah, well, that was great." He picked up his club and bag. "Thanks, boys, I'll stop by again tomorrow and let you know how it's going."

"Just one last thing," I said. "What's in the bag?"

"A couple of geese that got ka-bonged by golf balls," Roadkill Man said. "I can't wait to show them to Mrs. Roadkill Man. See ya!"

Roadkill Man left.

"Know what I feel really good about?" Justin asked.

"What?"

"Not only is Roadkill Man getting to play golf on a real golf course," he said. "But he gets to bring home dinner every night. I mean, this must be his idea of heaven."

For the rest of the week Roadkill Man practiced golf every day and went home every night with a couple of ka-bonged geese. He was starting to get holes in one. Now all he had to do was get one on Tuesday when the contest officially began.

"What do you get when you put a canary in a blender?" Justin asked Amanda and me on Sunday evening after dinner. We were sitting on the steps of the bunkhouse, enjoying the sunset.

Amanda and I both shook our heads. We'd given up trying to guess his jokes.

"Shredded tweet," Justin said with a grin. "What does Mozart do now that he's dead?"

"Do we really have to go through this?" I asked.

"Come on, guys," Justin implored us. "This is fun."

"For who?" Amanda asked.

"Aw, gimme a break," Justin said. "This one's easy. What does Mozart do now that he's dead?"

Again we shook our heads.

"He decomposes!" Justin said. "Get it? When he was alive he composed symphonies. But when he's dead, he *de*composes!"

"Have you noticed that Justin's jokes have gotten really morbid lately?" Amanda asked me.

"I wonder if it has something to do with that creepy book Terry's reading," I said.

"Hey, look." Amanda pointed over at the campers' cabins. "Isn't that Roadkill Man?"

She was right. Roadkill Man was looking around outside the cabins as if he was searching for something. He even got down on his hands and knees and peeked underneath a few of them.

"What's he doing?" Justin asked.

"He seems to be looking for something," I said. "Let's go see what's going on."

We walked across the grass. Roadkill Man was on his hands and knees, peering into the crawl space under one of the cabins.

"What are you looking for?" Amanda asked him.

"My golf club," Roadkill Man said, turning to us. He had a worried look on his face. "It's gone."

"You think someone took it?" I asked.

"The campers are always teasing me about my torn clothes and my old golf club," Roadkill Man said. "I'm hoping one of them hid it."

"Why are you hoping for that?" Justin asked.

"Because if they didn't hide it, then I really don't

have any idea where it could be," he replied, and looked under the next cabin.

"When did it disappear?" I asked.

Roadkill Man told us that he'd left the golf club near the first tee and had gone to collect a ka-bonged goose. When he got back, the club was gone.

Justin and I shared a worried look. Campers weren't allowed to go anywhere near The Blob's private course. That made it unlikely that one of the campers had taken the golf club.

"Just out of curiosity," Justin said, "do you have any other clubs?"

"No," Roadkill Man replied. "That's the only one I own. My grandpa gave it to me when I was young."

"Suppose we could find you another club," I said. "Could you use it?"

"Gee, I don't really know," Roadkill Man answered. "I haven't used another club in twenty years. It would probably take some getting used to." He looked toward the horizon. The sun had just gone down, and the sky was turning to dusk. "Mrs. Roadkill Man worries if I'm not home by dark. I'm gonna have to go. I hate to trouble you kids, but do you think you could ask around and find out if anyone's seen my club?"

"Sure thing, Roadkill Man," I said. "You go back home and don't worry about it. We'll find that club for you."

"Thanks, kids." Roadkill Man headed toward the dark woods.

As soon as he was out of earshot, Justin gave me a worried look. "What do you think?" he asked.

"I don't think a camper took that club," I said.

"You think whoever took it wants to make sure Roadkill Man doesn't win the hole-in-one contest?" Amanda guessed.

I nodded.

"Why do I think Schmook the Crook is somehow involved?" Justin asked.

CHAPTER 19

That night we waited until Terry got into bed and started to read. We got Bag to come talk to him with us.

"Uh, Terry, could we ask you a favor?" I said.

Terry looked up from his book. "What?"

"Did you know that more than fifty kinds of fish can produce musical sounds?" Justin asked.

Terry raised his eyebrows and gave him a perplexed look.

"Actually, we were wondering if we could have tomorrow off?" I said.

"Are you crazy?" Terry replied. "Who's going to cook?"

"The orphan Sherpas," Bag said hopefully. "They are being very eager to learn to cook."

"That's nice, Baggy, but the orphan Sherpas don't even have *names*," Terry said. "How am I going to know who is who?"

"We have been giving them names," Bag said. He got the six orphan Sherpas to line up shoulder to shoulder. "Here are being Eeny, Meeny, Miny, and Moe."

"That's four," Terry said, and pointed at the last two orphans. "What about them?"

"Larry and Curly," Bag announced proudly.

"Do they understand English?" Terry asked.

"Of course," Bag replied. "You can be asking them anything."

"Okay." Terry turned to the orphans. "Eeny, have you ever picked your friend's nose?"

Eeny swallowed nervously and glanced out the corner of his eye at Bag, who gave him an encouraging nod.

"I am being most sorry, sir," Eeny replied. "You can be picking your own nose, and you can be picking your friends. But you cannot be picking your friend's nose."

Terry nodded and looked satisfied. He turned to Justin and me. "Okay, you guys can have tomorrow off."

The next morning we borrowed a pair of binoculars from Amanda so that we could spy on Brad without him knowing it. Then we set out to follow him. At the beginning of the summer, Brad had lived in the bunkhouse with us. But after we learned that he was a spy for The Blob, we made his life so uncomfortable that he moved out of the bunkhouse and into a campers' cabin with an extra bed.

"There he goes," Justin whispered. We were hiding behind a tree near Brad's cabin. Brad left the cabin, and we followed. Besides caddying and doing The Blob's dirty work, Brad's other job was picking up and delivering The Blob's special meal orders. So we weren't surprised that the first thing he did was go to The Blob's house and get his breakfast order. In fact, it wasn't until midmorning that Brad had any free time.

In the meantime, I got an earful of dumb jokes.

"So where did the King of Russia keep his armies?" Justin asked.

"I don't know, Justin, where?" I said.

"In his sleevies." Justin grinned.

I made a fist. "One more lame joke and I kill you."

"Hey, look." Justin pointed at The Blob's house. Brad was coming out the front door, carrying a small golf bag.

"Now where's he going?" Justin asked.

"Looks like he's headed toward the golf course," I said.

"So he's gonna caddie for The Blob," Justin said.

"I don't think so," I said. "That isn't The Blob's golf bag."

Giving Brad plenty of room, we trailed him to the golf course. The course was already crowded with golfers practicing for the hole-in-one contest.

"Looks like he's going to practice for the contest," Justin said in a low voice.

But instead of joining the other golfers, Brad

walked past them and disappeared into the trees.

"Now where's he going?" Justin asked.

"I don't know," I said. "But maybe he'll lead us to Roadkill Man's golf club."

We followed Brad into the woods and discovered a trail. Brad was about fifty yards ahead.

"So why didn't the skeleton cross the road?" Justin whispered as we quietly trailed Brad.

"Not now, Justin," I whispered back.

"Aw, come on, just this one?" he begged.

"Okay," I sighed. "Tell me."

"Because he didn't have the guts," Justin said. "Why can't skeletons play music in churches?"

"I thought you said just one joke," I whispered.

"This is the second part of the same joke," Justin whispered back.

"Fine," I said. "I have no idea why skeletons can't play music in churches."

"Because they don't have any organs," Justin whispered.

"Hey, Justin," I said. "What do you and a headless skeleton have in common?"

"I don't know," Justin replied.

"Neither of you has a *brain*," I said. "Now be quiet. I don't want Brad to know we're here."

Ahead of us Brad left the woods and came out into a clearing. Justin and I followed him to the edge of the woods and hid behind some bushes. Brad stepped up to a golf tee.

"It's the eighteenth hole," Justin whispered. "The last one on the course."

The tee was empty. Brad put down the golf bag and took out a club and a ball.

"Why would he come all the way out here to practice?" I wondered.

"Who knows?" Justin said. "Maybe he's really bad and doesn't want anyone to see."

But then Brad reached into the golf bag and took out something else — a small black box with some knobs and a thin antenna sticking out of it.

"Hey, that sort of looks like the remote Ralphie was using to steer his toy truck," Justin whispered.

"Shhh!" I pressed my finger to my lips.

Over at the tee, Brad took a big swing and smacked the ball into the air. Then he dropped the golf club, quickly picked up the small black box, and began turning the knobs.

"I don't get it," Justin said. "What's he doing?"

At first I didn't get it, either. Then I had an idea and scooped up the binoculars. I focused them on the eighteenth green just as Brad's ball landed. The ball almost rolled to a stop, but then began to roll again, weaving a path . . . straight to the hole!

I lowered the binoculars in shock. "I don't believe it!"

"What?" Justin asked. "What is it?"

"Brad's got a remote-control golf ball!"

CHAPTER

Justin picked up the binoculars and watched as Brad took another ball out of the golf bag, hit it, and guided it to the hole with the remote control.

"It's Robo-Ball!" Justin cried in a low voice. "So that's what Brad's up to. He wants to win the million dollars!"

"And that's why he must have taken Roadkill Man's golf club," I said. "To make sure no one else has a chance."

"What a dirtbag," Justin grunted. "There's just one thing I don't get. How is he going to hit the ball and guide it with the remote control when all the other golfers are around? They'll all see him."

"Because *he's* not going to hit the ball," I said. "The Blob is."

"Huh?" Justin looked confused.

"They must be planning this scam together," I said. "Brad's hitting Robo-Balls now just to make sure they work. But in the actual contest, The Blob will hit the balls. Brad will be hiding out in the woods somewhere with the remote. He'll guide the ball in from there."

Justin shook his head in disgust. "It's a foolproof plan. They're bound to get a hole in one and win the million dollars. The Blob will get rich *and* he'll still be able to turn Camp Run-a-Muck into a golf resort."

"Maybe," I said. "But we may be able to stop him."

"**Y**ou want to borrow my mini Big Foot?" Ralphie asked. We were in his cabin, which looked and sounded more like a video arcade than a camp bunk. Bells and whistles rang from pinball machines, tinny music played from Mortal Kombat, and engines roared in video racing games. Two or three campers crowded around every game, cheering their buddies on.

Ralphie was hunched over the electronic insides of an old Terminator II game, welding some wires together with a small blowtorch.

"Not the truck, just the remote," I said.

"Why?" Ralphie asked.

Justin and I shared a look. We didn't want to tell him the real story.

"Uh, we want to play a trick on a friend," I said. "He's got a remote-operated racing car, and we want to take control of it when he's not looking."

"Well, it's not that simple," Ralphie said. "All these remotes work on different radio frequencies. They do that so that a bunch of guys can get together and race their cars without interfering with each other's controls. You can't override another guy's remote unless you know his frequency."

Justin's shoulders sagged. "That's a bummer, man. We'll never be able to find out what the frequency is."

"Well, there is one way to do it," Ralphie said. "If you had a remote with a frequency scanner, then you could lock into your friend's frequency and override it."

"So where would we get this scanner?" I asked.

"I don't know," Ralphie said. "I've never actually seen one. I just know they exist."

"Oh, great," Justin groaned.

"Listen, Ralphie," I said. "Just knowing scanners exist isn't gonna do us any good if we can't get one."

Ralphie tugged on his ear and seemed lost in thought. "Well, maybe I could build one."

"How long would that take?" I asked.

"Let's see," Ralphie said. "First I'd have to get the parts. Then I'd have to put the thing together. There'd probably be some welding involved. Then I'd have to test it. And then there's all the fine-tuning. So you'd have to figure a couple of weeks at least."

"We've got two days," Justin said.

Ralphie shook his head. "Sorry, guys, that's impos-

72

sible. There's no way I could build it that fast."

"Hey, Ralphie," I said. "How would you and your buddies like some real brick-oven pizza with fresh tomato sauce and cheese?"

"And a really delicious crispy crust," Justin added.

"And unlimited bottles of Coke," I said.

"Ice cold," added Justin.

At the mention of food, Ralphie's cabin buddies left their video games and swarmed around us like hungry buzzards.

"Real brick-oven pizza?" Ricky Pulger repeated with a glazed look.

"Unlimited Coke?" Another camper drooled.

Ralphie licked his lips and stared at Justin and me. "You guys are joking, right?"

"We're dead serious," I said. "Just build us that scanner."

"You gotta do it," Ralphie's buddies urged him.

Ralphie thought it over. "I have to be honest with you guys. I'd kill for fresh pizza, but I *still* don't think I could build a remote scanner that fast."

"Would you at least try?" I asked.

Before Ralphie could answer, Ricky Pulger said, "Hey, for real pizza and Coke, he'll do anything. Right, Ralphie?"

Ralphie nodded. "All I'm saying is, I can't promise."

"We'll all help," said another one of his friends. "I can get some guys from the other cabins, too."

"We can set up on the tables in the arts and crafts shack," said Ricky.

"Deal," I said, and started to get up.

"Wait," said Ralphie. "When do we get the pizza?"

"Tonight," I said. "And more tomorrow."

Ralphie grinned. "We'll get right to work."

We'd just left Ralphie's cabin and were heading for the bunkhouse when someone called our names. We turned around and saw Amanda hurrying toward us with a golf club in her hands.

"Look what I found!" she said. The club was all rusty and had a really strange-shaped head.

"Where'd you find it?" I said.

"I asked around," she said. "One of the girls remembered seeing it in a corner of her cabin. Turns out it's been there for years. Some camper from a long time ago must have left it."

"Thanks, Amanda," I said. "We have to go over to Log Cabin Pizza later to get some pies for Ralphie and his friends. We'll drop the club off at Roadkill Man's cave on the way."

Roadkill Man wasn't at the cave when we dropped the club off, but Mrs. Roadkill Man was. She was a big woman with flowers woven into her greasy gray hair and B.O. strong enough to rival her husband's.

"Hello, boys!" she called cheerfully from the cave kitchen where she was cooking.

"Hey, Mrs. Roadkill Man," I said. "Congratulations. We hear you're gonna have a baby."

Mrs. Roadkill Man patted her big tummy and beamed proudly. "Three months to go and then our big bundle of joy will finally be here."

"Hey, that reminds me of a joke," Justin said.

"Oh, good," Mrs. Roadkill Man said. "I just *love* jokes."

"Did you hear about the mommy cat who swallowed a ball of yarn?" Justin asked.

"No."

"She had mittens!" Justin said.

Mrs. Roadkill Man burst into peals of appreciative laughter. "Tell me another one, please?" she begged.

"Uh, okay," said Justin. "Here's a riddle. When is a car not a car?"

"I don't know," said Mrs. Roadkill Man.

"When it turns into a driveway," Justin said.

Mrs. Roadkill Man held her belly and laughed. It was hard to believe, but it looked like Justin had finally found someone who liked his dumb jokes.

"Want to hear another one?" Justin asked.

"I'd love to, but I'd better not," Mrs. Roadkill Man said, wiping the tears of laughter out of her eyes. "If I laugh any harder, I'm afraid I might hurt the baby. But thank you for brightening my day. And thank you so much for entering my husband in the hole-in-one contest. Even if he doesn't win, we've really been enjoying the geese he brings home."

I noticed a big jar on the kitchen counter filled with greenish liquid. Black things floated around inside it.

"Mind if I ask what this is?" I said.

"Pickled goose feet," Mrs. Roadkill Man replied. "Would you like to try some? They're a delicacy, and absolutely delicious."

"Oh, uh, thanks," I said, not wanting to hurt her feelings. "We're on our way to get a pizza, and I wouldn't want to spoil my appetite."

"I understand," Mrs. Roadkill Man said. "But feel free to stop by anytime and have some. You boys have been so good to Roadkill Man and me. And we'd like to show you our appreciation."

"Thanks, Mrs. Roadkill Man," I said. I turned to leave, but Justin stopped and asked her if she wanted to hear just one last joke.

"Oh, okay, just one," Mrs. Roadkill Man replied.

"Why were the little strawberries so upset?" Justin asked.

"I don't know," replied Mrs. Roadkill Man.

"Because their parents were in a jam!" Justin said.

"He-he-he-he-he-hah!" Mrs. Roadkill Man laughed heartily.

"Looks like you've found a friend," I said to Justin as we left.

"Yeah." Justin nodded and smiled. "It's good to know that *someone* around here has a sense of humor."

CHAPTER

23

For the next twenty-four hours we supplied the pizzas and Coke while Ralphie's buddies scoured the camp for the parts needed to build a frequency scanner. He and his friends had taken over the arts and crafts shack and turned it into a workshop.

Each time Ralphie needed another part, he stood up on a chair and shouted, "Okay, listen up, guys, I need something dish-shaped for the antenna."

"How big?" one of the campers asked.

Ralphie spread his arms to show how large he thought it should be.

The campers were out the door in a flash. Ralphie climbed down from the table and went back to work. The table was covered with pieces of electronic junk — everything from flashlight parts to game gear to a small laptop computer.

"How's it going?" I asked.

Ralphie shook his head. "I don't know if we're

gonna make it in time. It's hard to get the right parts."

By now we'd told him the real reason why we needed the scanner.

"You have to do it, Ralphie," Justin urged him. "For the sake of Camp Run-a-Muck. For the future of the nation and our children."

Ralphie frowned at him. "I don't have any children."

"But it sounds good, doesn't it?" Justin asked.

A kid jogged into the workshop. He was breathing hard and carrying the rounded bottom of an outdoor barbecue grill.

"Think this'll work as the dish antenna?" the kid asked.

Ralphie looked it over and smiled. "Yeah, this'll be perfect!"

It looked sort of familiar to me. "Can I ask where you got it?"

The kid shot Ralphie a nervous look out of the corner of his eye.

"It's cool," Ralphie said. "These guys are on our side."

"I took it from the big yellow and white house behind the camp," the kid said.

Justin's jaw dropped. "The Blob's house?"

"I don't know who lives there," the kid said with a shrug.

"Listen, dude, that's the owner of the camp,"

Justin said. "If he finds out you took his grill, he'll — "

Before Justin could say anything more, I gave him a nudge and whispered, "Chill out. Desperate times call for desperate measures." I turned to the kid. "Good work. Take your reward."

The kid went over to the pizza box and took out two slices. "Hey, it's cold!"

"Throw it in the pottery kiln for a minute," Ralphie said, without looking up from his work.

Justin tugged me over to a corner. "I don't like this, man," he whispered. "If The Blob ever finds out we're taking his stuff, he'll grind us up and feed us to The Blob Dog."

"Yeah, but look at it this way," I whispered back. "If the plan works, The Blob will be history. If the plan doesn't work, *the camp* will be history. Either way, it's not gonna matter."

The door to the workshop swung open, and Road-kill Man stepped in. His shoulders sagged, and he dragged the rusty golf club behind him.

"Bad news, boys," he said. "I tried this club all afternoon. I can't hit a thing."

CHAPTER

24

"**M**aybe you just have to keep practicing," I said.

Roadkill Man shook his head. "It's not gonna work. I've played all my life with my grandpa's old wooden golf club. I can't switch now."

Like a huge dark cloud, a sense of gloom descended over the arts and crafts shack. If Roadkill Man couldn't get a hole in one, we'd lose Camp Run-a-Muck. It grew quiet as Ralphie and his buddies hung their heads.

The door opened, and Amanda came in. "Hey, guys," she said brightly. "How's it going?"

"Not good," Justin answered with a heavy sigh.

"What's the problem?" she asked.

We told her how the old rusty club she'd found wasn't working for Roadkill Man.

"We might as well give up," Justin said. "I mean, what's the point of trying to build the frequency scanner? Even if we stop Brad and The Blob, we'll still be nowhere."

Ralphie reached up to the industrial lighting hanging over the worktable and turned it off. The arts and crafts shack grew even gloomier.

"I guess it's not too soon to start thinking about what we're gonna do next year when there's no Camp Run-a-Muck anymore," he said.

"I'm really sorry, guys," Roadkill Man said. "I mean, I'll really miss you."

The arts and crafts shack grew still, as if no one had the heart to say anything more. With his shoulders sagging, Justin trudged toward the door. "Guess we'd better get back to the kitchen," he moped.

"I can't *believe* you guys." It was Amanda, with her hands on her hips. She blocked the doorway.

Justin looked up, surprised.

"How can you give up like this?" Amanda demanded. "How can you let Brad and my uncle win? Just because we can't find Roadkill Man's club? I mean, haven't you learned *anything* from your experience here at Camp Run-a-Muck?"

"I can't think of anything," Justin said, scratching his head. He turned to me. "What about you, Lucas? Have you learned anything?"

I shook my head.

"I learned that a cockroach can live for more than two weeks without its head," said Ricky Pulger.

"I learned that the heart of a giraffe is two feet

long and weighs almost twenty-five pounds," said another kid.

"An elephant's trunk is operated by more than forty thousand muscles," volunteered a third.

"That's not what I'm talking about," Amanda said. "I'm talking about having faith. I'm talking about never giving up. I'm talking about pushing ahead when it looks like there's no hope."

"You learned *that* at Camp Run-a-Muck?" Ralphie asked, amazed.

"Well, no, but I thought it sounded good," Amanda admitted. "You have to keep working on that scanner, Ralphie. Justin and Lucas, I know you have to get back to the kitchen, but you also have to keep supplying everyone with pizza."

"But my club," Roadkill Man said.

"We'll organize a search party," Amanda said. "In the meantime, Roadkill Man, I know you don't like that old rusty club, but you have to keep trying."

"But there's no chance," Roadkill Man said.

"Maybe not," said Amanda. "But maybe, when the time comes, you'll get lucky."

CHAPTER
25

Thick dark clouds hung over the camp the next morning. The Defungo Extra-Strength Deep-Pit Deodorant $1 Million Hole-in-One Contest was about to begin. Justin and I had spent the previous day working in the kitchen and keeping Ralphie and his buddies supplied with pizza. In the meantime, Amanda had organized half the camp to look for Roadkill Man's club.

Justin and I headed for the arts and crafts shack to see how Ralphie was doing on the scanner.

The shack looked like a disaster area. Exhausted campers were asleep on the floor. Empty pizza boxes and soda cans were scattered everywhere. We found Ralphie with his head buried in his arms at the worktable. He was fast asleep.

"Hey, Ralphie." I shook his shoulder gently. "Better wake up, bud."

"Huh?" Ralphie looked up with dazed, bloodshot eyes. "What happened?"

"Nothing yet," said Justin. "But the contest is gonna begin anytime now. How's the scanner?"

Ralphie yawned. "See for yourself." He swept his arm over the table, which was covered with hundreds of electronic parts.

"All I see is parts," I said.

"What you see is what you get," Ralphie said with another yawn.

"Parts?" Justin said. "What are we gonna do with parts?"

"Guess I have to put 'em together," Ralphie said, rubbing his eyes. "Give me an hour."

"I don't think we've got an hour," I said. "The contest is gonna begin anytime now."

"Tell me where you'll be," Ralphie said. "I'll get there as soon as I can."

I told Ralphie we'd be in the woods near the first hole. Then Justin and I left the arts and crafts shack and started toward the golf course. Above us the dark clouds were thickening.

"Looks like rain," Justin said.

"Yeah." I nodded. "Why aren't I feeling good about this?"

"Uh, because the contest is about to begin and we don't have a frequency scanner?" Justin guessed. "And even if Ralphie finishes the frequency scanner, we don't have Roadkill Man's favorite golf club. And without his golf club, he can't get a hole in one, anyway. So I'd say you have a pretty good reason for not feeling good about this."

As we crossed the camp and headed for the golf course, a large banner came into view:

WELCOME TO

THE DEFUNGO $1 MILLION HOLE-IN-ONE CONTEST,

SPONSORED BY

DEFUNGO EXTRA-STRENGTH DEEP-PIT DEODORANT

"SINK THAT MIGHTY STINK WITH DEEP PIT"

The banner hung from a platform about ten feet high. On the platform were a bunch of men with binoculars.

"They must be the contest judges," Justin said.

Under the banner, dozens of golfers in brightly colored golf outfits were milling around, waiting for the contest to begin. And standing off to the side was Roadkill Man.

"Peace, dudes." He gave us a sad smile. "Any sign of my grandpa's club?"

I shook my head. "Not yet. Don't give up hope, Roadkill Man. Maybe we'll get lucky. Maybe lightning will strike."

Roadkill Man looked up at the dark clouds. "Well, I'm pretty sure lightning is going to strike. But what does that have to do with my club?"

Before I could explain, a man in a blue suit stepped up to a microphone on the platform and began to speak to the crowd: *"Good morning, ladies and gentlemen, and welcome to the Defungo $1 Million Hole-in-One Contest. My name is Brody Odifer and, as Mr. B.O., the spokesman for Defungo Extra-Strength Deep-Pit Deodorant, I will be your host for today's contest."*

Brody Odifer, or Mr. B.O., as he preferred to be called, went on to outline the rules of the contest. Each player would get ten balls and have ten chances to hit a hole in one. The contest would be observed by judges on the platform as well as by two additional judges near the cup.

"And without further ado, would the first contestant tee up," Mr. B.O. announced. *"That will be Mr. Joseph Petrol, of New Castle."*

A golfer wearing a sky blue polo shirt and bright green slacks put a ball on the first tee, lined up his shot, and swung. *Thwack!* The ball shot way up into the air and headed for the green, but missed the hole.

"Come on," I said to Justin. "Let's head for the woods."

"Just a second." Justin turned to Roadkill Man and raised his hand in a fist. "Keep the faith, brother."

Roadkill Man raised his hand in a fist. "Power to the People."

We headed into the woods. "What's the point?" Justin asked. "Ralphie hasn't shown up with the

scanner. Amanda hasn't found Roadkill Man's favorite club. We're totally out of it."

"Maybe, but I still want to watch," I said.

We walked into the woods, but it seemed pretty
hopeless. I knew Justin was right, but I didn't want
to admit it. With Roadkill Man out of the contest,
we'd never win the one million dollar prize and never
be able to buy Camp Run-a-Muck from The Blob. It
really did look like it was time to start thinking about
doing something different next summer.

"Ooof!" Just then I bumped into Justin's back. He
must've stopped in the woods. I'd bumped into him
because I wasn't paying attention.

"Hey, what is it?" I asked.

"Look," Justin whispered. Brad Schmook was coming toward us through the trees.

CHAPTER

26

When Brad saw us, he stopped. "What are you guys doing here?"

"What are *you* doing here?" Justin asked back.

Brad's eyes darted around nervously. "Well, uh . . . look, I've been trying to tell you guys something for days, but you never give me the chance."

"That's because we know you, and we know whose side you're on," Justin said.

Brad shook his head. "No, you don't. You really don't know me at all. Because you never give me a chance to say anything."

"You're right," said Justin. "And you want to know why? Because actions speak louder than words. And so far this summer, *every* action from you has been a scam that dumps on the campers."

"Okay, maybe that's true," Brad admitted. "But maybe I've changed."

Justin rolled his eyes in disbelief. "You're so full of

89

it. Come on, Lucas, let's get out of here before Brad the Cad starts telling us how he's changed his ways and become a new person."

Brad pressed his lips into a thin, flat line and looked really frustrated.

"Can you believe that guy?" Justin muttered as we continued through the woods toward the green.

"I can't figure him out," I said.

"Oh, come on, Lucas," Justin scoffed. "It's easy. Can't you see that he's just trying to be friendly so we won't suspect him when The Blob gets his Robo-Ball hole in one?"

"I guess," I said, but I really wasn't certain.

By the time we got to the hole, the first contestant had used up his ten shots. He hadn't made a hole in one, and the judges were picking his golf balls off the grass. The judges all had disgusted looks on their faces and I could see why. A bunch of geese had been hanging around the tee, eating grass and leaving goose poops everywhere. Every ball that hit near the tee inevitably rolled over some goose poop and turned slimy green.

"Contestant number two!" Mr. B.O.'s voice blared over the microphone. *"Ms. Camellia Monroe. Tee up and take your shots!"*

Justin and I settled down in the woods just off the edge of the golf course to watch. We heard a distant *Thwack!* as Ms. Monroe drove her first ball toward the hole.

Thump. The ball landed on the green about twenty feet from the hole and rolled off to the left.

"Not even close," Justin whispered.

For the next hour, contestant after contestant took his or her turn at the tee and tried to hit a hole in one. Some came pretty close. Others missed by so much that Justin and I had to duck as the golf balls caromed into the woods around us. Meanwhile, the clouds above us grew thicker and darker.

"Man, it is definitely going to rain," Justin whispered.

"Time for our next contestant," Mr. B.O.'s voice blared over the microphone. *"Mr. Robert Kirby."*

"It's The Blob!" Justin hissed. "And look!" He pointed to the trees on the other side of the green. Someone was moving around in there.

"It must be Brad with his remote," Justin whispered.

Just then, I heard the rustling of leaves and twigs behind us. I turned around. Ralphie was staggering toward us, dragging a big black thing that looked like a barbecue grill with a pole sticking straight out of the middle.

CHAPTER

27

"I'm not too late, am I?" Ralphie whispered, letting go of the scanner.

"Depends on how fast you can set this thing up," I whispered back. "It's The Blob's turn right now!"

Thwack! In the distance we heard a ball tee off.

"That's his first shot!" Justin gasped.

"I'll set it up as fast as I can." Ralphie started to scramble.

Meanwhile, we heard a crackling sound as The Blob's first Robo-Ball sailed into the woods, breaking branches and bouncing off limbs. It fell to the forest floor about a dozen yards away from us. Suddenly it started to roll toward the green.

"Get it!" I whispered to Justin.

Staying low, Justin scurried through the underbrush and pounced on the golf ball. Then he crawled back toward us.

"Where is it?" I whispered.

92

"In my pocket." He patted his jeans pocket. "Good thing it didn't get any goose poop on it."

Thwack! The Blob hit his second shot. This ball landed in the rough at the edge of the trees. It, too, started to roll.

"Grab it!" I hissed.

Once again Justin scurried through the trees. He reached the edge of the woods, stretched his arm through the tall grass, and snagged the ball before it could roll toward the green. Then he scampered back to us.

"Man, that was close," he whispered. "The judges almost saw me. If The Blob hits a Robo-Ball any closer to the green than that, there's no way I'm gonna be able to get it."

I turned to Ralphie. "How much longer till the scanner is ready?"

"A minute, maybe two," Ralphie whispered back.

"Hurry!"

CHAPTER
28

Luckily The Blob's next two shots were so far off that they landed in the woods behind us.

"Don't worry about those," Ralphie whispered. "They're too far away for Brad's remote to reach them."

Thwack! The Blob hit yet another Robo-Ball.

We held our breaths and kept our fingers crossed, hoping that ball would also sail out of range.

Thump! It landed on the green!

"It's thirty feet from the cup!" I said in a low voice.

The next thing I knew, Ralphie pointed at the barbecue grill. "Quick," he whispered. "Aim it at the ball!"

I tried to pick up the grill, but it weighed a ton. "Jeez, what's the story with this thing?"

"It's loaded with old car batteries," Ralphie said. "I had to find a strong power source."

I grimaced and managed to pick it up. I pointed it

at the ball, which had begun rolling toward the cup. Meanwhile, Ralphie was sitting on the forest floor with a laptop computer and a pair of earphones on.

The ball was twenty-five feet from the cup and moving steadily.

"Can't you stop it?" Justin asked anxiously.

"Shhhh! I have to get the frequency first." Ralphie tapped the keys on the laptop.

Now the ball was twenty feet from the cup.

"Come on, come on!" Ralphie growled at the laptop.

Fifteen feet and rolling.

"For Pete's sake!" Ralphie typed quickly. Justin and I shared a dismal look.

The ball was ten feet from the pin and turning green as it rolled through goose poop.

"Aw, man, now what?" Ralphie glared at the laptop. Then he banged it with his hand.

"It's five feet!" Justin whispered urgently.

Ralphie ignored him. He was totally focused on the laptop.

"Four feet," Justin said.

"Three feet . . ."

"Two feet . . ."

"One foot!"

"Come on, Ralphie," I whispered.

Ralphie's fingers flew over the keyboard. Suddenly I felt the grill vibrate and hum.

"What's happening?" Ralphie whispered.

"It's six inches from the hole," Justin hissed. "But I think it's stopped."

Ralphie kept typing. The grill kept vibrating.

"It's starting to roll away!" Justin said.

Ralphie had a big grin on his face. Feeling relieved, I put the barbecue grill down.

"Hey!" Justin cried. "It's starting back toward the hole again!"

"You have to keep the grill aimed," Ralphie told me.

I hauled up the grill again.

"It's headed away from the hole!" Justin sounded relieved.

With me aiming the grill and Ralphie working the laptop, we guided The Blob's ball into a sand trap.

Thump! A second later, another Robo-Ball landed on the green and started to roll toward the hole.

"That's The Blob's sixth shot!" Justin whispered.

Once again Ralphie and I guided the ball into a sand trap.

"How come the ball obeys us and not Brad?" I asked.

"Are you kidding?" Ralphie chuckled. "Brad's got a dinky little remote running on double-A batteries. We've got Mega-Grill running on a twelve-volt car battery power plant. Our setup is ten times more powerful than his."

Thump! Thump! Thump! Three more shots

landed, and three more times we guided The Blob's balls into the sand trap.

Thwack! In the distance we heard another shot.

"That has to be The Blob's tenth and last shot," Justin whispered.

Thump! The ball hit the green and started to roll toward the hole. Ralphie's fingers were a blur over the laptop.

But the ball was still rolling toward the hole!

"Hey, something's wrong!" Ralphie gasped.

CHAPTER

29

"**W**hat's the problem?" I asked.

"I'm not sure," Ralphie said as he typed in a flurry. His forehead was wrinkled. "Brad couldn't have switched frequencies on us. Somehow he's strengthened his signal."

"Look!" Justin pointed at the green. Brad had come out of the woods and was actually standing over the last Robo-Ball, guiding it toward the hole with his remote.

"Darn!" Ralphie muttered. "He's right on top of the ball! Lucas, you have to get the Mega-Grill closer!"

"But I thought our signal was stronger," I said.

"Sure it is," Ralphie said. "But he's much closer to the ball. The closer you are, the stronger your signal appears. He's overriding us."

"He's five feet from the hole and closing!" Justin yelled.

"Go!" Ralphie yelled at me.

"Where?" I asked.

"To the green," he said.

I lugged the Mega-Grill out of the woods and toward the green. By now the Robo-Ball was only three feet from the hole, and Brad was moving it closer. I got between the hole and the ball and aimed the Mega-Grill. The ball started to roll away from the hole.

"I figured you guys were behind this," Brad grumbled. He pushed his remote closer to the ball. It started back toward the hole. Meanwhile, it was getting covered with a thick layer of green goose poop.

"Cheaters never win, Brad," I said, pushing the Mega-Grill closer to the ball. Once again, it started to roll *away* from the hole.

"You don't understand," Brad said, getting down on his knees and holding the remote just inches from the ball. "I tried to tell you, but you wouldn't listen."

"What's to understand?" I asked, placing the Mega-Grill just inches from the other side of the ball.

The Robo-Ball rolled back and forth between the two remotes as if it couldn't make up its mind.

Tweeeeeeet! Suddenly a whistle blew. A Defungo Extra-Strength Deep-Pit Deodorant judge ran toward us waving a red flag.

"Disqualification!" he shouted.

"Sorry, folks," Mr. B.O.'s voice rang out over the microphone. *"It appears we have a disqualification due to illegal ball tampering."*

A golf cart bounced along the fairway toward us and skidded to a stop, leaving long skid marks on the green. The Blob jumped out. His face was red with anger.

"What do you mean, I'm disqualified?" he shouted at the Defungo Extra-Strength Deep-Pit Deodorant judge.

The judge held up the slimy Robo-Ball with his fingertips. The ball was almost completely green. The judge had a disgusted look on his face. "We have reason to believe that this ball has been tampered with. I'm confiscating it and sending it back to the lab for analysis."

"The heck you are," The Blob growled, and grabbed the goose-poop-covered Robo-Ball out of the judge's hand. Before the judge could stop him, The Blob popped the ball in his mouth and swallowed.

"Aw, gross!" Justin moaned.

"I'm gonna barf!" Ralphie groaned, and turned away.

Even Brad the Cad winced.

"You've got no evidence now," The Blob said triumphantly.

"Actually, he does," Justin said, taking the two Robo-Balls out of his pocket that he'd grabbed at the beginning of The Blob's turn. He handed them to the judge, who quickly put them in his own pocket.

"Well, Mr. Kirby," the judge said with a smile, "I

guess I'll be on my way to the lab to look at these balls." And before The Blob could say another thing, he left.

Seething with anger, The Blob looked around for someone else to aim his wrath at. His sights settled on Brad.

"You idiot!" The Blob screamed at him. "How could you let them have those balls? You boneheaded nitwit! You just cost me a million dollars!"

Lightning flashed, and thunder rumbled above us. I felt a raindrop land on my shoulder. Then another. Then it started to pour.

"Ladies and gentleman," Mr. B.O. announced over the microphone. *"We will have a rain delay until further notice."*

CHAPTER

30

We all ran through the rain back to the arts and crafts shack. Inside, everyone traded high fives.

"We did it!" I shouted happily. "We stopped The Blob and his Robo-Balls!"

"We just cost him a million bucks!" Ralphie whooped gleefully.

"And he ate a Robo-Ball covered with goose poop!" Justin added.

"Did you see the way he lit into Brad the Cad?" Ralphie asked me. "Was that cool or what?"

"Yeah," I said with a halfhearted shrug, and glanced at Roadkill Man, who was standing quietly near the door.

"Hey, what's wrong with you?" Justin asked me.

"We may have stopped The Blob from winning the million bucks," I said. "But without Roadkill Man's favorite golf club, we don't have a shot, either."

Everyone got quiet.

"He's right," Ralphie said. "And without that million bucks, it's good-bye Camp Run-a-Muck."

"Maybe we just got lucky," Justin said. "I mean, with this rain delay we still have time to look for Roadkill Man's club."

Just at that moment, the door to the arts and crafts shack opened, and Amanda came in wearing a yellow rain slicker. Rainwater dripped from the hood and sleeves.

"Any luck?" I asked hopefully.

She shook her head. "We've looked everywhere. I mean, there are millions of places where that golf club could be."

"Including the bottom of the lake," said Ralphie.

"Maybe we're going about this the wrong way," I said. "I mean, we *know* Brad took it. Instead of searching all over the place, maybe it's time to get Brad to tell us where it is."

Justin shook his head. "He'll never tell us."

"Maybe I could get him to tell," Amanda said. "I mean, we all know he has a crush on me."

"I'm not sure it'll work," I said. "We used that trick to get him to eat mutilated monkey meat. It's hard to believe he'd fall for it again."

Ralphie pushed open the arts and crafts shack door and looked outside. "I'm not sure it's gonna matter, guys. The clouds have passed, and the sky's starting to turn blue."

He was right. Even though the rainwater was still

dripping from the roof and the trees, the sun was out.

"*Ladies and gentlemen,*" Mr. B.O.'s voice boomed out over the microphone. "*We apologize for the rain delay. The Defungo $1 Million Hole-in-One Contest is now ready to resume. The remaining competitors should return to the first hole.*"

I gave Roadkill Man a grim look. "Might as well give it your best shot."

CHAPTER 31

We all walked over to the golf course together. Mrs. Roadkill Man was there with her jar of pickled goose feet, and so was Terry, Bag, and the orphan Sherpas, along with all the kids from Amanda's search party.

A lady wearing a white sun hat, a lime green polo shirt, and a plaid skirt was taking her turn at the tee. She came close a couple of times, but couldn't get a hole in one.

"Well, ladies and gentlemen, so far no one has been able to get a hole in one," Mr. B.O. announced over the microphone. *"We have one contestant left. A Mr., er, Roadkill Man . . . hmmm, interesting name. Anyway, would Mr. Roadkill Man please come to the first tee."*

Roadkill Man turned to the rest of us with a hopeless look.

"Give it your best," Amanda said encouragingly.

"You can do it, honey." Mrs. Roadkill Man gave her husband a kiss on the cheek.

"When the going gets tough, the tough go golfing," said Ralphie.

"Try to get in touch with the inner Roadkill Man," suggested Terry.

"It is important to be believing in yourself," Bag said.

"And if you can't get a hole in one, at least get a goose," added Mrs. Roadkill Man.

Roadkill Man forced a grin onto his face. He picked up the rusty club and headed for the first tee.

Most of the other golfers had already left. Once their turn was over, they weren't interested in seeing if anyone else won. But the few who remained chuckled and whispered to each other when they saw Roadkill Man set up his first ball on the tee. He lined the ball up with the rusty club.

Thwack! The ball shot high into the air, hooked left, and disappeared into the woods.

Roadkill Man sighed and shook his head as if it was hopeless. He teed up his second ball.

Thwack! This one took off like a line drive. *Bonk!* It hit a tree on the other side of the course.

I traded a dismal look with Mrs. Roadkill Man and Terry. We could see that Roadkill Man was trying his best, but it was still no good. So far not a single ball had even come close to the hole. Up on the platform, the contest judges were shaking their heads and packing up their bags.

Thwack! Thwack! Roadkill Man tried again, and again.

It wasn't long before he had one shot left.

He teed up the ball.

He steadied the rusty club and pulled it back.

"Wait!" a voice shouted.

We all turned. Brad Schmook was running toward us with something in his hands.

"I don't believe it!" Amanda said.

Justin rubbed his eyes. "I must be seeing things."

"Is it my imagination, or is this being part of a fairy tale?" Bag asked.

No one knew what to say as Brad arrived, out of breath, with Roadkill Man's old wooden club in his hands.

"Why are you doing this?" I asked.

"I kept trying to tell you, but you wouldn't listen," Brad said. "I love Camp Run-a-Muck. I don't want to see Mr. Kirby turn it into a golf resort any more than you do."

Justin shook his head. "Then why did you try to help The Blob with those Robo-Balls?"

"He forced me to," Brad said. "I didn't have a choice."

"Bull," said Terry. "I think this is a trick."

"Let me ask you guys a question," Brad said. "If

this is a trick, who put the entry fee for the hole-in-one contest under Justin's pillow?"

I felt my jaw drop. "That was *you?*"

Brad nodded.

"*Excuse me,*" Mr. B.O. announced over the microphone. "*Mr. Roadkill Man has one shot left. And frankly, we'd all like him to take it so we can go home.*"

Brad held out the old wooden club to Roadkill Man. "It's in your hands now."

Roadkill Man looked down at his hands, which were still empty because the club was still in Brad's hands. "Well, actually, it's still in *your* hands."

"That's not what I meant," Brad said, handing him the club.

Roadkill Man stepped up to the tee and positioned his last ball.

"*Well, folks,*" Mr. B.O. said with a chuckle. "*It appears that the delay was so that Mr. Roadkill Man could switch from an old rusty club to an old wooden one. As if that will somehow make a difference.*"

Roadkill Man brought the club back.

Everyone crossed their fingers.

Roadkill Man swung.

Thwack! The ball shot high into the air and straight down the fairway.

"*And that brings the Defungo $1 Million Hole-in-One Contest to an end,*" Mr. B.O. announced. "*On behalf of myself and the Defungo Company, we'd like to thank all the contestants —* "

A loud murmur rose from the judges on the platform. One of them hurried over to Brody Odifer and whispered something in his ear.

"What?" Mr. B.O. said, not realizing the microphone was still on. *"Are you serious? That scuzz-ball hippie got a hole in one? I don't believe it! Well, if ever there was someone who needed Defungo Extra-Strength Deep-Pit Deodorant, it's him. . . ."* He cleared his throat. *"Ladies and gentlemen, I have incredible news! A hole in one has just been scored!"*

A wild cheer went up from the campers and kitchen staff. Mrs. Roadkill Man hurried to her husband and hugged him while Roadkill Man raised his fists in triumph.

"Yes, folks, it's true," Mr. B.O. announced excitedly. *"Mr. Roadkill Man has won a million dollars from the Defungo Company and will appear this year in Defungo Extra-Strength Deep-Pit Deodorant ads. And now Mr. Igot Defungo, president of the Defungo Company, will present Mr. Roadkill Man with his check."*

Cameras flashed as a tall, handsome, red-haired man shook hands with Roadkill Man and handed him a huge cardboard check made out for one million dollars.

"On behalf of the Defungo group of companies," Mr. Igot Defungo said, "representing the complete line of Defungo Deodorants, Foulette Mouthwash, Itchytoze Athlete's Foot Cream, and Fartaway Air

Fresheners, I am delighted to present you with this check for one million dollars, and a free case of Defungo Extra-Strength Deep-Pit Deodorant." Mr. Defungo took a deep sniff and then wiped the tears from his eyes and added, "Which you definitely need."

Roadkill Man accepted the check and the deodorant with a frown. The photographers' cameras flashed.

"Is something wrong?" Mr. Igot Defungo asked.

"Don't you have anything smaller?" Roadkill Man asked.

"I'm sorry, I don't understand," Mr. Defungo said.

"Well, don't get me wrong," Roadkill Man said, looking down at the big cardboard check. "I really appreciate the million bucks. It's just that there's no way I can fold this thing up and get it into my wallet."

Mr. Igot Defungo smirked. "Don't worry, this is just for the cameras. The real check will fit into your wallet."

"Oh, gee, thanks." Roadkill Man grinned.

CHAPTER

33

Once the photographers were finished and the De-fungo people had gone, we kept celebrating Roadkill Man's triumph. By now the word had spread through the whole camp, and everyone was there. Everybody was patting Roadkill Man on the back and congratulating him.

"I still can't believe you did it," I told him. "I mean, when it came down to it, you had one real shot. Just one chance . . . and you made it!"

Roadkill Man smiled sheepishly and stroked his old wooden club. "This is what made all the difference."

Justin turned to Brad. "I guess I owe you an apology."

He held out his hand. Brad shook it.

"I still don't understand why you did it," Justin said to him. "I mean, why'd you come over to our side?"

"I told you," Brad said. "I really love Camp Run-a-Muck. I don't want to see it go."

"But you didn't have to help us," I said. "You probably could have figured out a way to win the million dollars for yourself. Then you could have bought the camp."

Brad shook his head. "I'm tired of being the bad guy. I wanted to show you that I could do something good, too." As he said this, his gaze settled on Amanda. "I mean, now that I've helped Roadkill Man buy the camp, maybe I could get that kiss on the cheek?"

Amanda thought for a moment, then shook her head.

Brad looked disappointed, but Bag patted him on the back. "Don't be feeling bad, my friend. Always be remembering that virtue is being its own reward."

"Talk about rewards," Justin said. "We'd better get Roadkill Man to sign that check over to The Blob before someone changes their mind."

"He's right," I said. "The Blob's word isn't worth the bad breath its spoken with."

Amanda looked around at the departing golfers. "Where is he, anyway?"

CHAPTER

34

The Blob was nowhere in sight.

"I've got a funny feeling about this," Justin said, glancing at Brad.

"Don't look at me," Brad said. "If he's up to something, I don't know anything about it."

"Come on," I said. "Let's go to the house."

We all hurried to The Blob's house. A big crowd of campers followed us.

Justin and I knocked on the front door of the big yellow-and-white house.

No one answered.

"Guess he's not here," Justin said.

But I wasn't ready to leave. "This doesn't make sense. If he's not on the golf course or in the house, where could he be?"

"There he is!" Ricky Pulger pointed around the side of the house. The Blob was carrying a suitcase and hustling toward his car.

"Stop him!" I shouted.

CHAPTER

35

A crowd of campers ran over to the car and blocked The Blob's path.

"Out of my way, you whiny little punks!" The Blob shouted.

But nobody budged. Now that they knew Roadkill Man was going to buy the camp, they didn't have to listen to The Blob anymore.

"Aren't you forgetting something?" Justin asked as he, Roadkill Man, and I made our way through the crowd of campers.

"Not that I know of," The Blob replied.

"Roadkill Man has a check for a million dollars," Justin said. "And you agreed to sell Camp Run-a-Muck for that."

"Well, I've changed my mind," said The Blob.

"But you gave us your word," Justin said.

"Who cares?" The Blob growled.

"Excuse me for asking this," I said, "but why

wouldn't you sell this junky camp to us for a million bucks?"

"I wouldn't give you sniveling, slimy kids the satisfaction," The Blob snapped. "Not for all the money in the world. Now get out of my way!"

But the campers wouldn't budge.

"Okay," The Blob fumed. "If you won't let me get to my car, I'll go back to my house."

But the campers had crowded all around him and wouldn't let him move in that direction, either.

"So what are you gonna do?" The Blob asked with a laugh. "Attack me?"

"No one's going to attack you," Terry answered. "But we're not going to let you go anywhere, either. Not until you keep your word and sell Camp Run-a-Muck to Roadkill Man."

The Blob crossed his arms and sneered meanly. "Fine, we'll all just stay here and wait to see who gives up first."

Justin, Amanda, Roadkill Man, Terry, and I huddled.

"Looks like a standoff," I said in a low voice. "What can we do?"

Everyone shrugged or shook their heads.

Then I felt someone tap me on my shoulder. It was Ralphie.

"Sorry to interrupt," he said. "But I think I know a way."

CHAPTER
36

Ralphie told me to follow him. We left The Blob surrounded by campers and went back to the woods near the first hole.

"What are we doing here?" I asked.

Ralphie pointed at the Mega-Grill. "You gotta help me carry this back to The Blob's house."

"Why?" I asked.

"Remember what The Blob did with the disqualified Robo-Ball?" Ralphie asked as he strained to pick up the Mega-Grill.

"He swallowed it," I said.

"Right." Ralphie smiled.

I started to see what he was planning.

We carried the Mega-Grill back to The Blob's house. The Blob was still outside, surrounded by the campers.

"Hey, where'd you get that?" he asked when he saw me carrying the grill.

"We borrowed it from you," I said.

"Nobody gave you permission," The Blob huffed. "Now put it back!"

"In a moment," I said, aiming the Mega-Grill at him. "Now for the last time, are you going to sell Camp Run-a-Muck to Roadkill Man or not?"

A big smirk appeared on The Blob's face. "Get stuffed, kid."

I turned to Ralphie and nodded. He began to type quickly on the computer keyboard.

"Aw, isn't that cute," The Blob scoffed. "A secret weapon."

But the smile slowly turned into a look of concern. The space between The Blob's beady eyes deepened into a *V*. "What the . . . ?"

He blinked.

Then his eyes bulged.

Then his cheeks puffed out and he had to clamp a meaty hand over his mouth.

Ralphie kept typing away. I could just imagine what the goose-poop-covered golf ball in The Blob's stomach must have been doing. Probably bouncing this way and that, then maybe forcing its way upward . . . or downward. In general, making The Blob feel like there was a wild slimy golf ball slamming around in his guts.

Phweeeeeep! Little squirty sounds were coming from The Blob's lower regions. That golf ball must've been doing a number on his digestive tract.

"Uuuuhhhhhggggg!" The Blob groaned and fell to his knees. His face was bright red.

I looked back at Ralphie and nodded for him to ease up.

"I was wondering if you'd reconsider selling the camp," I said.

The Blob nodded slowly. "Anything," he gasped. "Just make it stop."

"Where's the deed for the camp?" Justin asked.

"In my office," The Blob grunted. "The file cabinet."

"I know where it is," Brad said.

"Make sure you bring some pens," I told him.

Brad pushed through the crowd and went into The Blob's house. A moment later he came out, waving a white piece of paper.

I gave the deed and a pen to The Blob. "You sign the deed over to Roadkill Man."

Then I gave a pen to Roadkill Man. "You sign the check over to Mr. Robert Kirby."

A moment later it was done.

"Happy?" The Blob asked.

I was just about to say yes when Terry whispered in my ear that The Blob had recently taken the key to his private refrigerator back. I turned to the former camp owner.

"Now we want the key to your private refrigerator."

The Blob's jaw dropped. "Never!"

I turned to Ralphie and nodded. Ralphie quickly typed something on the laptop.

Phweeeeeep! Phweeeeeep! More little squirty noises seeped from The Blob. His eyes bulged, and his face started to turn red again.

"Okay, okay!" He quickly jammed his hand into his pocket and handed me the key. "Just let me go!"

I told Ralphie to turn off the Mega-Grill. Making more little squirty noises, The Blob struggled to his feet and staggered back toward his house. "Outa my way! I gotta get to the bathroom!"

While the crowd of campers slowly parted to let him through, I shouted, "Okay, everyone, listen up! Roadkill Man is the new owner of Camp Run-a-Muck!"

"Hail to Camp Run-a-Muck!" the campers shouted. "Long Live Roadkill Man!"

We all went back to the camp kitchen to celebrate.

"I just want to thank you guys for this," Roadkill Man said, carrying the case of Defungo Extra-Strength Deep-Pit Deodorant under his arm. "I always wanted to have my own camp. Next summer we're going to have a great time!"

Mrs. Roadkill Man came toward Justin and me, holding out the big jar filled with greenish liquid and pickled goose feet. "Boys, as a token of our appreciation, we want you to have this."

"Uh, gee, thanks." Justin took the jar, then turned to me and rolled his eyes.

Roadkill Man had to go because his wife was feeling tired after all the excitement, but our celebration lasted long into the night. We liberated The Blob's private refrigerator and served up a feast in the dining hall. As the campers wolfed down steak and veal and pasta, they cheered for Terry, Justin, Bag, and me.

"This stuff is great!"

"Yeah, I can't believe The Blob kept it all for himself!"

Justin and I stopped at the table where the kids from Ralphie's cabin sat. But Ralphie wasn't there.

"Where is he?" I asked.

"Out behind the dining hall, barfing," Ricky Pulger said.

"Huh?" We couldn't understand it.

Just then, Ralphie staggered up to the table. His skin had a greenish tint, and he was wiping his mouth on his shirtsleeve.

"I don't get it, Ralphie," I said. "Wasn't this food good enough?"

"It was great," Ralphie said. "It actually scored a *negative* five on the Ralphie Barf-O-Meter."

"Then how come you barfed?" Justin asked.

"Oh, man, I'm just so excited," Ralphie said. "And I *always* barf when I'm excited."

We were back in the kitchen preparing dessert when Amanda rushed in. "I just went past Uncle Bob's house," she said. "He's packed up his car to leave for good."

"Are you a little bummed?" Justin asked. "I mean, after all, he *is* your step-uncle."

"I know," Amanda said, "but he wasn't very nice to anyone, was he?"

Just then the door swung open, and The Blob himself stepped in. The kitchen went dead silent. He looked around with a blank expression on his face. "I've come for some food," he said. "I've got a long trip ahead and I'll need something to eat."

"Too late," said Terry. "We gave it all to the campers."

"Isn't there anything left?" asked The Blob.

I looked around the kitchen and saw Mrs. Road-kill Man's big jar of pickled goose feet lying on the counter.

"The only thing left is this." I picked up the jar and brought it to him.

The Blob peered into the murky greenish liquid and frowned. "What is it?"

"Uh, we're not sure," I said. "It was given to us as a present. All we know is that it's supposed to be a delicacy."

The Blob unscrewed the top of the jar and sniffed. "Hmmm, smells sweet and sour." He reached in and pulled out a pickled goose foot. Drops of the murky green liquid dripped off it and onto his shirt as he held the black-webbed foot up to his nose.

"Doesn't smell bad," The Blob mumbled to himself. He opened his mouth and nibbled at the webbed foot. "Hey, not bad, not bad at all."

The next thing we knew, The Blob picked up the jar and left, chewing happily on the rest of the goose foot.

"This calls for our favorite song!" Justin yelled. And we all sang:

"Great green gobs of greasy grimy gopher guts
Mutilated monkey meat
Chopped-up birdy's feet.
French-fried eyeballs rolling up and down the street.
Oops! I forgot my spoon!
The Blob is gone
The Blob is gone
He's eating pickled goose's feet
The Blob is gone!"

ABOUT THE AUTHOR

Todd Strasser has written many award-winning novels for young and teenage readers. Among his best known are *Help! I'm Trapped in Obedience School* and *Girl Gives Birth to Own Prom Date*. He speaks frequently at schools about the craft of writing and conducts writing workshops for young people. He and his family live outside New York City with their yellow Labrador retriever, Mac. His next project for Scholastic will be *Help! I'm Trapped in Obedience School Again*.

IT'S A GUT-BUSTING GROSS-OUT!

CAMP RUN-A-MUCK #1

TODD STRASSER

YOU NEED *GUTS* TO EAT HERE!

When Justin and Lucas snag summer jobs as assistant cooks at Camp Run-a-Muck, there's only one problem: They have no idea how to cook! But when the despicable Camp Director Bob "The Blob" Kirby hogs the best food for his own private bar-b-que, the duo create *their* own recipe for revenge: Switch the hamburger meat for The Blob's cookout with ground-up dead gopher meat!

Camp Run-a-Muck #1: Greasy Grimy Gopher Guts

DON'T MISS
#2 Mutilated Monkey Meat
#3 Chopped Up Birdy's Feet

CRA11196

AVAILABLE WHEREVER BOOKS ARE SOLD